Nails in the Coffin

Robert Coburn

A Jack Hunter Mystery

ABSOLUTELY AMAZING eBOOKS

Habent Sua Fata Libelli

ABSOLUTELY AMAZING eBOOKS

Manhanset House
Shelter Island Hts., New York 11965-0342

bricktower@aol.com • tech@absolutelyamazingebooks.com
• absolutelyamazingebooks.com

Library of Congress Cataloging-in-Publication Data
Coburn, Robert
Nails in the coffin
p. cm.

1. FICTION / Mystery & Detective / Private Investigators. 2. FICTION / Thrillers / Crime. 3. FICTION / Thrillers / Suspense
Fiction, I. Title.
ISBN: 978-1-955036-32-0, Trade Paper

December 2021

Nails in the Coffin

Robert Coburn

A Jack Hunter Mystery

Other books by Robert Coburn

A Loose Knot

A Deadly Deception

The Pink Gun

Little Boxes

Bad Tidings

An Evil Number

Malice Murder

A Rage of Deaths

Dead Drop

Acknowledgments

Once more, my eternal thanks to my wife, Laura, for her tireless and tough editing. And a special thanks to my friend and publisher, Shirrel Rhoades, for taking a chance with me.

Chapter 1

The sun rose out of the Florida Straits to flash a blinding eyeshot across South Roosevelt Blvd. Morning traffic was light. Only two vehicles heading north, a hearse and a black Lincoln Navigator following close behind.

The hearse driver squinted and reached to pull down the sun visor. He didn't see the shovel lying in the road right in his path. The left front tire exploded with a concussive boom and the hearse suddenly lurched across the center line into the oncoming lane, its steering wheel spinning wildly and breaking the driver's thumb.

Jack Hunter had rounded the bend by the old houseboat row and was passing the Key West airport in his red Jeep. He was returning from the Stock Island marina where the *Joyful Noise* was docked. He'd been spending a few nights on her. It would've been shorter to have taken North Roosevelt but he liked driving along the oceanside. He was making good time nevertheless on the empty road. Remarkably, he hadn't seen a single vehicle until this very moment, when suddenly one caromed across the road and flipped over in front of him. He slammed on the brakes screeching to a stop.

A coffin flew out of the back door of the tumbling hearse and skidded into the Jeep, lodging itself solidly beneath the front end. The Lincoln Navigator had stopped in the middle of the road and its driver jumped out and ran over to the hearse, which had come to rest right side up. He jerked open the door and shook the unconscious driver, who was slumped in the seat. Unable to revive him, he pulled a gun from his waist and shot the man pointblank in the head. Then he looked over to where Jack sat dumbfounded in the Jeep not twenty feet away, his hands still gripping the steering wheel. The Lincoln's horn began to blare nonstop. The shooter pointed the gun at Jack, took aim and then grinned. He jammed the gun back in his waist, spat at Jack and ran back to the waiting car.

Jack watched it speed away.

~~~

Detective Earl Gleason showed his badge to the officer manning the road block at Bertha Street and was waved through. He could see a jumble of patrol cars and an ambulance up ahead, all with roof lights madly flashing. Both sides of the road had been closed. As he neared the scene of the accident, he also spotted another vehicle in the mix which gave him pause. A bright red Jeep. He pulled over and got out.

"What've we got, Sgt. Fallows?" he asked, walking up to the officer.

The first responders had radioed for a sergeant to come to the scene after determining that a possible homicide might be involved. The sergeant had called Gleason.

"A real doozy, detective," Fallows said. "You'll have to see for yourself."

Gleason gave him a curious look and both men walked together to the battered hearse.

"How's the foot?" Fallows asked.

Gleason still had a slight hitch in his step resulting from a fractured metatarsal bone.

"Taking forever and a day to heal," Gleason said sourly.

The driver's body sat tilted to the right, held in place by the seat belt, an obvious entry wound in the left temple. Gleason leaned in through the open door for a closer look. Blood splatters on the passenger door window cautioned him that it wouldn't be a pretty sight to examine the exit wound.

"Was the door open when the officers arrived?" he asked, backing out and straightening up.

"Yes, sir. Everything's like they found it."

"Okay, leave it just as it is. Don't let anyone touch the door. I want to secure this scene. You're in charge. Get the photographer out here. Have a video made, too. Who reported this?"

"It's kind of complicated," Fallows said. "Guy who owns that Jeep claims he told a passing motorist to call 911 since he didn't have a phone. Everybody has a phone, so who's he kidding? Anyway, the motorist left before patrol arrived. We have the Jeep's driver twiddling his thumbs in the back seat of a patrol car."

Gleason looked at the Jeep and shook his head in disbelief.

"He said the hearse overturned right in front of him," Fallows went on to explain. "Next thing he knows some guy jumps out of a SUV that'd stopped on the other side of the road, runs up to the hearse, shoots the driver, gets back in the SUV and drives off. We've put out an APB to the sheriffs but nothing back so far."

"Do you believe him?" Gleason asked. "The Jeep guy?"

"I don't know what to believe," Fallows said. "Seems like he's telling the truth. On the other hand, it could've been road range gone bad. Actually, that kind of makes more sense when you think about it. The whole SUV business sounds fishy to me. The guy was vague about describing it other than he thought it was black. No idea of make or model. Like I said, there hasn't been any news from the sheriffs following our APB. Not surprising since they have so little to go on. Can't very well put up a roadblock along the entire Keys and stop every black SUV that comes along. We haven't found a gun. He could've tossed it in the ocean, I suppose. We'll have a diver search along the shore line. There is a .40 caliber brass casing on the road surface near the hearse. We've marked the location. Photographer can grab a shot of it before we bag it. But there's something else you should see, detective."

They walked around the hearse and over to the Jeep where a metal coffin was jammed under its front end.

"Jesus Christ," Gleason muttered. "Is there a body in that thing?"

"We don't know. Waiting for a hazmat team from the fire department to get here before we try to move it. Probably need a tow truck to pick up the Jeep off of the thing. My guess is the coffin must've flown out of the hearse during the crash. Guess it wasn't wearing a seatbelt."

"Okay, same drill with the coffin," Gleason said, ignoring the joke. "Nobody touches anything without wearing gloves. Where's the patrol car with the Jeep's owner?"

"Parked at the curb over there. Want to see him?"

"Yeah," Gleason said, giving another shake of his head. "If it's who I think it is, you won't need to call a diver to look for any gun."

The sergeant led Gleason to the car and opened its back door.

"Hello, Earl," Jack smiled. "How's the foot?"

Chapter 2

The hearse driver's body had been taken to the morgue at the Lower Keys hospital, as had the damaged coffin after it'd been dragged out from under the Jeep. The hazmat technician had decided the morgue would be a better place to open it rather than at the scene. The wrecked hearse was trucked on a flatbed to the police impound yard and the Jeep was towed to a repair garage at Jack's request. With all the hullabaloo, it was nearly noon before South Roosevelt Blvd. could be opened to traffic.

"I thought he was going to shoot me," Jack said nervously and grinned. "The weird thing is I must've been too scared to be afraid. Just sat there like a dumb ass. Then the SUV's horn started blowing like crazy and he lowered the gun. My lucky day, I guess."

He was talking with Gleason in an interview room at the police station. The detective had driven him there after finishing up at the crime scene.

"I won't argue with that," Gleason said grimly. "You okay? Seeing someone shot and the next thing the gun's being pointed at you can mess with your head. Not trying to be funny here. Bad guy once drew down on me, thought I'd shit."

"Didn't want to mention that part," Jack laughed. "And then he spits at me, for Christ's sake. No, actually I'm not okay. Still kind of shook up. I've been in dangerous spots before, it'll pass. Just have to give it the time."

"That is interesting, his doing that," Gleason mused. "Spitting at you. Freaky. Think you could give a decent description of him? We can put together a composite."

"I'll do the best I can."

"What about the SUV?" Gleason asked. "Anything coming back on it?"

"Total blank. Like I told the cops, the only thing I remember is it was black. Which is what every other one you see is."

"All right. This thing's going to be all over the news. Since you're a key witness, it'd be better for the investigation if you don't talk with any reporters. We'll keep your name out of it on our part. Nothing I can do about the people who called it in. You said it was a man and a woman?"

"Yeah, she was upset. Didn't want to hang around. They'd arrived after everything was over anyway. The SUV was long gone."

"All right, I'll check with the operator's log just to tie up that end."

"Found out who was in the coffin yet?"

"Waiting to hear from the from the hazmat tech at the morgue. There're a lot of protocols to follow before you pop the top off a coffin. What's the latest on my favorite and former detective, Rachel Powers?"

"I haven't heard from her for awhile."

"She was a good cop," Gleason said. "Hated to see her go. Miss her."

Jack didn't reply.

Gleason's phone rang.

"Homicide. This is Detective Gleason."

"Hello, detective," a bright voice replied. "This is Tim Davis. I've opened the coffin."

Davis was with the fire department's Rescue 1 unit, which provides rescue assistance and hazmat service. They'd answered the police request for help.

"What have you got?" Gleason asked.

"Nails in a coffin," Davis chortled.

"Come on, Davis," Gleason said impatiently. "Cut the funny stuff. I haven't got time for this crap."

"I'm serious, detective, it's full of what I believe are some badass drugs."

"You mean they're in there with the body?"

"There's no body in the coffin. You better get someone from narcotics over here."

~~~

Gleason had excused Jack, saying he'd make arrangements for him to meet with the sketch artist later. Now he was in a waiting room at the morgue with Detective John Cawben from narcotics and Tim Davis.

"Put these on, one over the other," Davis said, giving both detectives two pairs of gloves. "Much safer than the kind you normally use. Made with a tighter mesh. I'll tell you how to dispose of them after we're finished."

Gleason and Cawben exchanged glances as they slipped on the gloves.

The three men entered another room outside of the actual morgue where the coffin rested on a gurney. Its top was open and a white canvas duffle bag was inside.

"What the hell is that supposed to be?" Gleason muttered.

"I'm guessing about fifty or so kilos of fentanyl," Davis said. "We recently had a seminar on drugs. Stuff's transdermal and can be absorbed through the skin. That's why the gloves. You can also inhale it, so don't get nosey, ha, ha."

Cawben ignored the joke and walked over to the coffin, reached in the bag and pulled out a large zip-lock bag full of tablets.

"The marking on the pills looks right," he said. "You have any idea of how many people this much fentanyl could kill?"

"I know it doesn't take much," Gleason said, coming over to take a look for himself.

"Two milligrams are lethal for most people," Cawben explained. "That's so little you'd hardly be able to see it. Fit under your pinky fingernail. You've got enough here to take out every single person in the state of Florida. Maybe the good folks in Georgia and Alabama as well."

"What's the plan, detectives?" Davis asked.

"It'd be too dangerous to take this stuff back to the station the way it's packaged now," Cawben said. "I wouldn't trust it. Should have secondary packaging and a heat sealed bag for each ziplock. And even then I'm not sure we'd want this much fentanyl lying around in the evidence room."

"So what do you recommend?" Gleason asked.

"I'm going to have the crime scene photographer come here and document everything as it is in place," Cawben said. "Then we'll spread out the ziplock bags on a table and document them both together and individually."

"And after that?" Gleason asked.

"The lab will want to analyze it to make sure it's what we believe it to be. We'll get them a sample from each bag. Also, they might be able identify its origin. Eventually our hazmat friends will destroy the crap. But first, I want to get a court approval before we do anything. And Mr. Davis here will need to sign an affidavit."

"What about the coffin? Do the hazmat people get rid of it, too?"

"That's a good question, Earl. Technically, it's evidence in a homicide so it should belong to you. The only problem is the thing could be contaminated. What do think about that, Mr. Davis?"

"I didn't see any bags that were torn so nothing has spilled out. You'd probably be safe but have some Naloxone handy. That'll keep you alive until the medics get there."

Gleason wasn't sure how much he appreciated the last remark but he let it go.

"I want the coffin taken to our impound garage when you're finished here," he said.

"Thought you might," Cawben said. "I'll call for patrol to send someone here to watch this place before we all leave. Thank you for your help, Mr. Davis. And don't worry, I'll make sure there's plenty of Naloxone available when we return."

Chapter 3

Jack had walked home from the police station. As he'd turned into his lane, memories flooded his mind.

How the neighborhood had immediately appealed to him. And after moving in discovering that while everyone living there was friendly enough, they also respected each other's privacy. Well, up to a point. Things *had* gotten a little dicey once with a neighbor. She'd tried to kill him. In the end everything had worked out—if not to her satisfaction, certainly to his.

The good memories faded to the present. Now he wasn't at all sure of where his life was headed. His sojourn at the marina had failed to provide any direction.

He mounted the steps and went inside.

It was stuffy and smelled a little moldy. He was surprised. The house hadn't been shut up all that long. He threw open a couple of windows and grabbed a beer from the refrigerator. After this morning, he could use a cold one.

He took the beer into the living room and flopped down on the sofa. He thought again of the man pointing a gun at him. He raised his own finger as if to point back and mouthed 'bang.' Then the entire bizarre event replayed from start to finish. He was still rattled. He wondered who the poor driver had been. He'd never seen anyone murdered before. And with such cold and mechanical intent.

He took in a deep breath and reached for his cellphone on the side table where he'd left it. He had decided to stay completely off the grid when he'd gone to the boat. Not the smartest move he'd now come to realize.

Blessedly, there weren't many messages. Three from Billy Bean. One from his office in Los Angeles and one more from the dock master at the Stock Island marina. He saw that it had come in earlier that very morning. He played them back starting with Billy's.

The first one said they should replace the kitchen stove at the Inedible Cafe. What was that all about, he wondered? It had already been replaced after the old stove almost burned down the restaurant. The next two had to do with a band named the Troubled Birds that he thought they should book for the Undrinkable Bar. Billy's in the music business now?

The LA call brought pleasant news. His real estate company had forgiven rent payments from several businesses that leased space in an office building he owned. They were good tenants and he wanted to help keep them afloat during the coronavirus crisis. Now they were on their feet again and repaying the back rent.

The dock master said a guy was interested in buying his boat. Did he want to sell it? Well, that was the thing, wasn't it? He'd never considered the *Joyful Noise* as being *his* boat even though he'd bought and paid for it. As far as he was concerned it belonged to Bobby Sunshine and always would. He'd get back to the dock master. Right now he had other matters on his mind.

He finished his beer and went to the back porch to get his bicycle.

~~~

Key West had taken a financial beating during the off and on shutdowns during the pandemic. Many locals who'd lived here for years had left town. Businesses had closed and jobs had dried up. The island was slowly getting back on its feet once again. There were still more than a few vacant store fronts but some venturous souls had reopened. And some of the second- and third-vacation-home owners had returned from their main residences up north. Tourism was on a modest rise. But it would be quite a while, if ever, before things got back to what they once were. It was simply up and down as you go. And one day at a time.

Jack rolled his bicycle into the alley behind the Inedible Cafe and went inside through the kitchen door.

"Thought you'd quit riding that thing," Billy said disapprovingly. "'Course that old Jeep's not much safer, hee-hee."

"Jeep's in the shop," Jack said. "What's all this stuff doing out of the refrigerator?"

A dozen or so whipped cream canisters were sitting on a table. Jack picked up one.

"Careful with that, Jack!" Billy cautioned, taking the canister from him and placing it back with the others. "Throwing those things out before somebody gets hurt."

"Don't think they're spoiled do you?" Jack asked. "An expiration date's printed on the label."

"Nothing to do with spoiling," Billy said gravely. "Read in the paper today where a whipped cream canister blew up and killed a lady over in France."

"That's got to be a spoof," Jack laughed, stepping away from the table nonetheless.

"Wouldn't be in the paper if it wasn't so," Billy said defensively. "Police think something was wrong with the little gizmo on top you push to get the cream out. Suppose to be looking into that with the fellow who makes the cans. Said they'd stopped selling them back in 2010."

"Billy, that was years ago," Jack said. "Even if it did happen, why are you worrying now?

"This is Key West, Jack. People lose track of time here. So what's that ol' Jeep doing in the shop? Besides spending your money, hee, hee."

"Had an accident this morning."

"Hope nobody was hurt," Bill said with concern. "You okay? What happened?"

"A coffin ran into me."

Billy let that settle for a moment.

"That's a good one, Jack," he chuckled. "Anybody in that coffin I might know, hee, hee?"

"It wasn't a joke, Billy. This really happened. A hearse turned over right in front of me as I was driving past the airport and a coffin fell out and skidded under the Jeep."

Jack then told him the entire story. After he'd finished, Billy suggested they go out to the bar and have a drink. Jack agreed and put the whipped cream canisters back in the refrigerator.

~~~

"The victim's cellphone is a cheap burner," Gleason said. "Criminals like them because they're hard to track down. They're usually tossed after a few calls. Our vic obviously hadn't finished with his. Officer Ed Stone is the new tech specialist. He's away right now. Due back tomorrow. I'll get him to check it out."

He was in Lt. Jay Halderman's office. The lieutenant headed homicide at KWPD.

"I've logged everything else into the evidence room but I'm holding on to the phone in case we get a call," Gleason continued.

"What about the victim?" Halderman asked. "Local person?"

"From California," Gleason said. "Something familiar about him, too. Can't put my finger on it. Bugging the hell out of me. Here's a copy of his drivers license. Take a look."

"Carl Napier," Halderman read aloud. "Address here says he lives in Encino. Know where that is, Earl? I've never been to California."

"Los Angeles area," Gleason said.

"Odd him being from California and driving a hearse in Key West," Halderman said.

"Everything about this case is odd," Gleason said. "The hearse is registered to a funeral home in Miami. Got the telephone number. I'll call them next. Just wanted to update you on what we have. I'll also check with Los Angeles PD. You remember Detective Laura Dalton? She's a friend of Jack Hunter's. Worked with us on a case once. I'll get her to run Napier."

"I do remember her," Halderman said. "Thought of stealing her for us but she wasn't too keen on that idea. By the way, the newspaper's pretty upset that their reporter couldn't get to the scene. Been hounding me all morning."

"Not surprised. I told Jack Hunter to keep his mouth shut. Don't know how long that will last. He was shaken up about nearly becoming a victim himself."

"So what's next, Earl?"

"I better get back to work making some phone calls."

At his desk, Gleason first put in a call to Mike Green in Miami. Green was a DEA agent he'd met regarding a major drug dealer who'd been spotted in Key West. Unfortunately, the suspect had slipped away before they could arrest him. The call went to voicemail so he left a message detailing what it was about.

His next call was to the funeral home. They picked up.

"Christo Mortuary," a woman's voice announced pleasantly. "This is Carrie Talick. How may I help you?"

"Good afternoon, ma'am. My name is Detective Earl Gleason. I'm with the Key West Police Department and I'm calling about an accident involving a hearse owned by your company."

"Key West? I'm not aware of our hearse being there. When did this happen?"

"This morning. I have the vehicle registration."

Gleason read off the information, including the plate number.

"Well, I'm looking at our records here and that's certainly our hearse but I don't understand what it was doing there. It was parked in the drive when I left work yesterday. Was anyone injured?"

"The driver's at the hospital, ma'am."

Gleason purposely didn't say he was in the hospital morgue. He'd wait until he knew more about what was going on.

"Oh, poor Jimmy! Is he all right?"

"They are seeing to him," Gleason said. "You said his name is Jimmy?"

"Yes, James Rivera. Everybody calls him Jimmy. Nicest man. I'm so sorry this has happened. His wife's in a nursing home. Dementia. I know he wouldn't want to upset her."

Gleason paused.

"Is there another driver?" he asked. "A substitute you might've used?"

"As far as I know, Jimmy's the only one. But I've only been working here for a little over a month. So I guess there could be someone else they use."

"I'll need to speak with the owner," Gleason said. "May I have his name and could you connect me?"

"Jules Flores. He's out of the office today but will be back in tomorrow around noon. Would you like to leave a message?"

"No, I'll call him then. Thank you."

He checked his watch and saw it was going on to late afternoon in Los Angeles. He dialed the LAPD number for the Van Nuys division.

~~~

Jack stood at the end of Front Street facing the Key West Bight. The spot offered a spectacular view of the marina with rows of expensive yachts berthed along its piers. Jack, however, was feeling adrift.

He chained his bicycle to a bike rack and joined the promenade along the harbor boardwalk.

The crowd had already begun to thin, most people leaving for the sunset show at Mallory Square. He meandered along the dock with his thoughts for company. Familiar names painted on the sterns of the boats brought back memories. Many pleasant and others not. Yet all woven into the life he had made for himself and had come to enjoy on this quirky little island.

He could almost imagine Astrid Kelly's sailboat tied up a few piers over. For just a second he wondered if it might actually be. He let that thought pass.

The Schooner Wharf Bar was packed and a band was playing. The music caught Jack's ear and he went in.

Three women held the stage and they were knocking down the place. The guitarist was the vocalist. The drummer and bass player backed her up. It was solid rock but from a few of the licks Jack could tell they had also stood in the shadow of the blues. He liked their sound.

"What's the name of that group?" he asked the bartender.

"They're called the Troubled Birds. Supposed to be from England. Talk funny anyway. Came down from Miami. What can I get you?"

"I'm okay for the moment. Thanks."

He stepped outside to wait for the band to take a break. Billy had mentioned something about them in the phone message. He'd forgotten to ask when he saw him. He'd better start getting his head screwed on straight.

~~~

"Van Nuys Homicide," a woman's voice said over the phone.

"Is this Detective Laura Dalton?" Gleason asked.

"This is Dalton. How may I help you, sir?"

"Detective Earl Gleason here in Key West. We worked together one time when you were visiting. How are things in the big city?"

"Detective Gleason, of course," Dalton said. "Didn't recognize your voice. Good to hear from you. We're busy as ever to answer your question. What can I do for you?"

A chilling uneasiness came over her. Had something happened to Jack?

"I've got a homicide," Gleason said. "Really weird case. I won't go into the details other than drugs are involved. Victim has a California drivers license that gives a Los Angeles address. Town of Encino. Thought that might be near you. I'd like to know if he has any priors and was wondering if you could run him for me. Just trying to avoid getting tangled up in the system."

Gleason had decided not to mention Jack's involvement.

"If he has a record it's in our computers but sure, I don't mind." Dalton said, feeling a sense of relief. "Give me what you have."

"His name is Carl Napier."

Gleason then spelled out the name, read off the full address and drivers licenses number.

"Okay, got it," Dalton said.

"Almost forgot," Gleason added. "I believe you're due a belated congratulations on your engagement. Jack Hunter told me about it. When's the big day? Or has that already come?"

Dalton paused for a moment.

"We're taking a timeout at the present," she replied coolly.

"Oh, I'm sorry. I didn't mean to…"

"Don't worry about it. I'll get back to you as soon as I have something."

Gleason thanked her and hung up. No sooner had he done that than his phone rang with *I Shot the Sheriff.* Mike Green was returning his call.

Chapter 4

"His expression was stone-cold blank, when he shot the guy," Jack said. "Impassive. Like it was no big deal killing someone."

He was at the police station with Josh Golson, a sketch artist who lived in Islamorada and freelanced for different police departments. Gleason had called Jack first thing that morning to let him know that the artist would be there at noon and was expecting him. Then he left town himself to drive to Miami and meet with the DEA agent there.

"Yeah, that's more like it," Jack nodded. "There was also a scar along the bottom of his chin. Looked like an old one."

"You said he appeared to be in his mid-twenties?"

"No more than thirty. Like I said before, average build. Looked in good shape but not like he was a body builder. Wore his hair slicked back. Nice cut. Oh, and there was some kind of tattoo on the side of his neck but I couldn't make it out."

Jack was amazed at the details he'd begun to remember. It was as if his would-be assassin had come there in person to pose for the artist.

"How'd you get into the sketching business?" he asked.

"I've always liked drawing," Golson said. "Finally figured out a way to make some money at it. What about his eyes?"

"Nothing behind them," Jack answered with a slight shiver. "Dead eyes. Don't know their color other than dark. Like a shark's, come to think of it. I thought police artists did this stuff with a computer."

"Some of us do," Golson said. "You can also copy details from a facial feature catalog. Comes with all ethnicities. Like pieces in a puzzle. Mix and match. Just move things around until you think you've got the picture. But I like to listen to the witness and use my imagination as we go along. Let's color the eyes dark brown, okay?"

"Works for me," Jack said.

Golson made a few more finishing flourishes.

"How does this look?" he asked, turning the sketch pad to Jack.

It was as if his would-be assassin had indeed posed for the session.

"That's him," Jack said harshly.

"Great," Golson smiled. "You were a good witness. Makes all the difference, believe me. I'll get this to Detective Gleason. Want a copy?"

That caught Jack by surprise. Why would he want one? Still.

"Let me take a picture of it instead," Jack said, after a moment and pulling out his cellphone.

~~~

DEA Agent Mike Green had agreed to meet Gleason at Woody's, a tiny restaurant in Coconut Grove. It was near his office and would also be an easy drive from there to the funeral home in West Miami.

"How's your burger?" Green asked.

"It's okay," Gleason shrugged. "Burger is a burger."

They were sitting at a table on the patio.

"Should've gotten the fish sandwich," Green said, taking a big bite from his.

"Don't like fish sandwiches."

"Don't know what you're missing, Earl. People come here from all over for one of these things. World famous, believe me."

Gleason's phone rang. He saw it was a Los Angeles number.

"Better take this," he said, getting up and walking over to the side. "Hello, Laura."

"Hi, seems your victim, Carl Napier, was a bad boy. Had two arrests for DUI. Got the first one reduced to reckless driving. Must've known the judge. Doubt if that'd happen today. Second one stuck. Lost his license for six months. Moving on to bigger and worse things, he was busted for possession with intent. Holding a couple of kilos of cocaine. Lawyer got him off on a technicality, otherwise he was looking at doing time. That was a couple of years ago. Haven't heard from him since."

"That's terrific, Laura. Wonder if he has any family there? Have to notify someone."

"I'll have that done. Anything else we can do for you today, sir? We're always at your service."

Gleason felt a slight blush warm his cheeks.

"Could you send me his rap sheet?" he asked anyway. "I'm away from my desk right now."

"Already in the email. Included a booking picture from the last DUI arrest, too."

"Thanks. I owe you."

"It's on the house. Give me a ring if you're ever out this way."

"I'll be sure to do that."

Gleason hung up wondering if that were an invitation. He returned to the table.

"How'd you hurt your foot?" Green asked, noticing the slight limp.

"Sprained ankle," Gleason said, tired of the question. "That was the LA department. Had some information about my homicide victim. Turns out he was busted for dealing coke. Slick lawyer got him off the hook."

"What's your vic's name?" Green asked, finishing his sandwich. "Maybe he's done business in Miami that I'd know about."

"Carl Napier."

"Napier...Napier," Green mused. "Something's ringing a bell. Oh, yeah, the sailboat guy. He was with that woman. Coast Guard rescued their boat off the sandbar."

"Huh?"

"Friends of your buddy who owns the restaurant in Key West with the funny name," Green said. "You called me about seeing him and his girlfriend there with Eduardo Grubber, remember? Grubber was number one on our list."

"I'm losing my mind," Gleason laughed. "Yeah, I'd earlier seen the BOLO on Grubber. Dropped by the restaurant and incredibly, there was Grubber with his wife and those two people. Called you but they'd all split by then. But here's something else. The restaurant owner you're talking about is also a key witness in my homicide. He saw the shooting. Amazing he wasn't shot himself. The shooter just spit at him. Crazy or what?"

"Back during Miami's cocaine cowboy days he would've been shot in a minute," Green said. "Witness or not. But they keep the killings among themselves now. Let bystanders be bystanders. No need to draw extra heat. Better for business that way. As far as the man spitting at him goes, it was a sign of disrespect. Letting him know that he mattered so little that he wasn't even worth shooting. Lucky thing for your witness."

"Strange world," Gleason said. "Too bad Grubber hadn't sailed with the happy couple that night back then. You ever get him?"

"Yeah, but the case was dropped," Green said. "Witnesses suddenly disappeared. Don't think they were just spit on either. He shuttles between Honduras and Miami as free as a bird. He'll slip up one day. They all do eventually. You going to eat those fries?"

"You take 'em," Gleason said, sliding the plate to him. "By the way, the woman's name who was with Napier on the sailboat is Astrid Kelly. Funny thing, she tried to hit on me at the restaurant that night. She's a looker, too. But I don't know, bad vibes or something. Kind of scary, actually. Put me off, anyway."

"The Coast Guard said both of them were pretty screwed up," Green chuckled. "Being stuck on a sandbar all day will do that, I guess. Tell me about the fentanyl."

"All pills and packaged in ziplock bags. Forty-eight kilos worth stashed in a white canvas duffle bag. Like a seabag that sailors carry their stuff in."

"Interesting thought," Green said. "The whole thing's ingenious. Have to hand it to them, hiding the drugs in a coffin was pretty cool. No one's likely to look there."

"But what was Napier doing driving the hearse?" Gleason asked. "He'd have to be playing in a bigger league with that much dope."

"Well, he knew Grubber," Green suggested. "Could be he was working for him. Same for his girlfriend."

"Woman I spoke with at the funeral home told me there was only one regular driver but admitted there could be others," Gleason said. "She hasn't been there long. Still in training."

"Maybe Napier was the other driver," Green said. "He and his girlfriend brought the stuff in on her sailboat."

"Possible, I suppose."

"Fentanyl has been showing up in a lot of overdoses and deaths lately," Green said. "Users not realizing what they've bought is contaminated. Sloppy packaging. Some believe it's just accidental. But now we're beginning to suspect something more is going on. The cartels are expanding their market."

"Not quite sure I understand," Gleason said.

"They look at business the same way as anyone else. People using cocaine just once in awhile aren't as profitable as those who use it several times every day. So if you're in the illegal drug trade, how do you expand the market? One sure way is to make your product more addictive so that the casual user can't do without it and has to up his game. Fentanyl is fifty times more potent than say, heroin. Lace your product with fentanyl, set the hook even harder and the profit line goes through the roof. Return customers is what it's all about. The only downside is you might kill a few."

"That's about the most sinister thing I've ever heard," Gleason said, shaking his head in disgust.

"Like I said, it's all business, Earl. We've gotten word on a really big shipment of coke heading this way from Honduras. Probably already arrived, for that matter. Miami's not the drug smugglers paradise like it was during the 'eighties. Everything was coming here directly from South America then. Mexico's now the favorite route into the US. Doesn't mean Miami's out of the picture, however. Honduras is Columbia's pipeline to here. Grubber runs it. More likely with their government's blessing. In fact, we have a line on that."

"But what's Key West have to do with it?" Gleason asked.

"Mexico is a giant producer of fentanyl," Green said. "High quality. Cheap price. Key West is in shouting distance from Yucatan. Nobody would think twice about a nice sailboat making the trip there and back. Think nothing about someone carrying a duffle bag on and off the boat either. Ask your friend at the restaurant if he's seen them around. What was his name again?"

"Jack Hunter," Gleason said. "The human hurricane."

"How's that?" Green asked curiously.

"Private joke. Ready to visit that funeral home?"

Chapter 5

Jack found his postoffice box crammed full of mail. Well, he hadn't been there for days. He pulled out the letters and carried them to a table for sorting. Most went into the recycling bin. Advertisements, special deals on this and that. One for a hearing aid. He ripped that up and stuck a couple that were bills in his back pocket. And that was it. Nothing from Rachel Powers.

He'd been aware of a distancing in their relationship. It wasn't the miles that separated them. Their lives were now on separate tracks. They were bound to diverge at some point. But would they continue in that direction? That was the worry. He'd hoped for more earlier when they were together. To his credit, he hadn't pushed. Still, he didn't have to like what seemed to be happening now.

The newspaper reporter that'd called had been pushy. How'd the guy get his name, he wondered? Gleason had practically ordered him not to give any interviews. He assumed the department wouldn't have released his name. Sure, he'd told Billy but he wouldn't have blabbed to anyone about it. Would he? No, it had to have come from a source the reporter has with the cops. Maybe he should mention that to Gleason.

He got on his bike and peddled off to nowhere in particular, which is often the more interesting way to go in Key West.

His meandering took him to Fort Zachary Taylor. Leaving his bike in the parking lot rack, he walked out on the sandy strip of beach and down to the water's edge. He liked to think that on a clear day you could see Cuba from there. Maybe if you stood on a ladder. He sat down and let his imagination run.

There she was again, just beyond the horizon. The girl in the brief bikini lying on the beach in Cuba looking back at him. Flirting, no less. It was a mind game he had played the first time he'd been at Ft. Zack. Just as much fun now.

A sailboat passed between them. Only it wasn't in his imagination. It was really happening. Further, he believed he recognized the boat. He jumped to his feet and squinted to see better.

He could almost swear it was the *Justice*. He stood watching as the boat tacked eastward. It seemed that his life was taking one bizarre turn after another. How long had Astrid Kelly been in Key West? Was she leaving now or just out for a sail?

Then again, was it really her? Could he really be sure? Was his imagination now playing tricks on him? The boat was some distance offshore. He couldn't actually see the name painted on its stern. A few other people were on the beach. He was of a good mind to ask if they'd seen the sailboat. Just in case he was hallucinating.

Instead, he walked back to his bike. He remembered that Billy wanted to talk to him. He'd stop by the Inedible Cafe on the way home.

He glanced back toward the beach and the sea stretching beyond. It had to be her, he thought. No other sailboat looked quite like that one. He pinched himself to see if he was dreaming.

~~~

Jules Flores was lying. He was obviously afraid of something. Gleason decided to sweat him a little more.

"Tell me again why your hearse was sent to Key West?" he asked. "I'd have expected a mortuary there would've been involved."

Flores scowled and shifted in his seat.

Gleason smiled back. Carrie Talick had obviously told him about the accident and that he could expect a phone call from the police. Two investigators arriving at his door instead had to have been a little unnerving.

"Sorry if I wasn't clear," Jules Flores said testily. "It's a common practice in our business. For example, if a person's out of town when he passes, the family upon getting word would naturally contact their local mortuary to make arrangements for the funeral. That firm would either transport the body back home or contract with a mortuary where the death occurred. In this case we decided to take care of everything ourselves. Be less distressful for them."

"So you're saying a family here in Miami called you to pick up a departed loved one in Key West," Gleason said. "Okay, that sounds reasonable. Do you have their name?"

"Sorry?"

"The family in distress who called you. I'd like their name."

"I'd have to ask for their permission first," Flores replied with a smarmy smile. "People are sensitive about that sort of thing. Could open us up to liability. Certainly be upsetting to them at the least."

"Well, I can appreciate respecting peoples' privacy and their feelings but I will need to know," Gleason said. "How about the mortuary's name for now, then?"

"I beg your pardon?"

"The mortuary where you picked up the anonymous soul in Key West. I wouldn't expect curbside service for that sort of thing."

"I've been out of town for a few days," Flores said, heaving a sigh and clearing his throat. "Unfortunately, I wasn't involved in making those arrangements."

"Who would've been responsible then? Is that person here?"

"I'm afraid she no longer works for us," Flores said. "The position has been consolidated. We're a small company. Business hasn't been all that great. In fact, we've been through some rough patches lately. I've had to cut overhead expenses wherever possible. Laid off most of our full-time staff. Just bring someone in when we need to."

Perhaps he should've started cutting overhead with himself, Gleason thought, taking in the man's fashionable well-fitting suit and the very expensive gold watch on his wrist. But Flores was bullshitting. He'd bet money that Flores got rid of Carrie Talick for another reason. He wouldn't pursue that for the moment, however.

"Back to the body still wasting away in Key West," he said. "What happens now? Funeral coming up and all. I'd imagine the family will be concerned. Possibly even upset."

"I don't see any need to bring the family into this situation at their time of grief, detective," Flores smiled. "Once you tell me where our hearse is located, I'll contract with a local mortuary there and send someone to pick up the vehicle. Won't delay anything. Not for a minute. I must say, though, I am surprised they sent two detectives here over for a finder bender. Apparently, no one suffered any injury other than our driver, which as I understand, was minor."

"The driver would've been James Rivera," Gleason said. "Is that correct?"

"Jimmy's our driver, yes. Very dependable fellow. I've kept him on the payroll. His wife's in a nursing home and he needs the income."

"How would you describe him? Jimmy, that is. You see, there's been some confusion that needs to be cleared up."

"You mean how he looks?" Flores laughed. "What does that have to do with anything?"

"Bear with me, sir. How he looks would be fine."

"Well, it's not something I pay much attention to, frankly," Flores said. "Naturally you can understand. Let me think for a moment. He's shorter than me. I believe he's in his sixes. I'll have to check our personnel records to be exact. Has gray hair. Kind of on the chubby side. Does that help?"

"Very much," Gleason said pleasantly. "Anything else?"

"He's been complaining lately about having no energy," Flores said. "Don't know if that means anything as to what you're looking for. I told him he ought to get some exercise and lose a little weight. He laughed that off. Said old age was creeping up on him—he just needed to get some rest. I work out a couple of days a week at the gym myself. Offered to take him along. They have a program for seniors. Told him I'd pay for it, of course. But again, why do you need me to describe him?"

"Well, that's what's been causing the confusion," Gleason said. "The driver of the hearse in Key West, who is now resting in the hospital morgue, looks nothing at all like the man you just described. Adding to that, he has a different name."

"I don't understand," Flores mumbled, a slight quaver in his voice.

"Nor do I," Gleason said. "But to answer an earlier question, the reason I'm here instead of a traffic cop is that I am conducting a homicide investigation. Agent Green, however, is with the Miami Drug Enforcement Agency. He may have some questions regarding a different investigation he's conducting. Agent Green?"

"Just a couple, if you don't mind," Green said with a broad smile.

Chapter 6

Plaintive meowing flooded the staircase landing while Gleason fumbled for his apartment keys.

"All right, all right, Mitts," he said, unlocking the door and stepping through. "I hear you. I know your dinner's late."

Mitts was a six-toed cat he'd inherited from a case he had worked. It could've been an escapee from the Hemingway House. Twenty or so of them lived there.

"Long day," he told the cat, going into the kitchen and opening a can of food. He held his nose while dumping half of it into a bowl and took the smelly meal out on the deck. The cat, rumbling with purrs, followed with his tail held high.

Gleason went back inside and flopped down in a chair. He removed two printouts from his pocket. One was Carl Napier's booking photo from years back that Detective Laura Dalton had sent him. The other was an enlarged copy of Napier's drivers license photo and obviously more recent. He'd stopped at the station after driving back from Miami and picked them up.

He compared the two. The booking photo was the more complimentary one, though it was taken when he was younger. The drivers licenses picture, though more recent but generally always unflattering, showed a droopiness in the left side of Napier's face.

He examined the license photo more closely. The area around the eyes definitely sagged. Even the corner of the mouth was slightly turned down. He compared it again with the booking shot.

Something obviously had happened between the time when the two photos were made. An accident? Illness? Did that have anything to do this case? Probably not. Still, he made a mental note to mention it at the autopsy.

Jules Flores's role in the matter was more than merely curious. He'd seemed genuinely surprised over Napier having been the hearse driver. But that had quickly turned into apparent fear. Mike Green couldn't get another word out of him. He knew something about that fentanyl.

After they'd left, Green had speculated the mortuary could've served as a distribution center for the bagmen to deliver the drugs. Said it was even possible that Flores was unaware of exactly what was going on but that didn't mean he was completely innocent. Well, that remained to be seen.

Napier's cellphone came to his mind. A cheap burner. Once no longer needed, it's tossed. And for complete anonymity, the sim card is also wiped clean or removed. The phone could have a lot to tell. He'd get it over to tech first thing in the morning.

He got up from the chair and checked his watch. It wasn't all that late. Plenty of time to take a walk. The exercise would be good for his foot. And it was a pleasant night. Maybe even a glass of merlot at Vino's would be in order.

His cellphone rang.

"Gleason," he answered.

"Detective Gleason. This is Sam Merrill. I caught night dick again. Guess it goes with being the new kid on the block."

Merrill had drawn night duty at the police station. He was on call whenever an incident required a detective's presence at the scene. He'd recently joined KWPD, coming from the Tampa police department where he had worked homicide. Rachel Power's leaving had opened a slot.

"Sorry to bother you at home," he continued, "but there's a telephone ringing in your desk drawer. Been a couple of calls, actually. Thought you'd like to know."

"I'll be right there," Gleason said.

So much for that walk, he thought, grabbing up his car keys and hurrying out.

The ride to the station was uneventful. Light traffic. Very few people on the sidewalks. Key West was still mending.

"Slow night?" Gleason said, greeting Merrill who was sitting at a desk in the detectives room.

"The way I like 'em," Merrill replied. "No further calls on your private line, by the way."

Gleason gave him a tight smile and unlocked his desk drawer. Removing the cellphone, he looked to see if it had a caller display. Nothing that he could determine. Rather than mess with it himself and possibly screw up something, he'd wait until morning and have the techs check it over. Then he'd sign it back into the evidence room where it should've been all along.

He slipped the phone into his pocket. If it rings again tonight, however, he'll answer the damn thing.

"What are you reading?" Gleason asked, noticing a magazine on Merrill's desk.

"Scuba Diving," Merrill said. "You a diver?"

"Landlubber."

"I've been into diving for years. One of the reasons I took the job here. You can't beat the water in Key West. Tampa doesn't even come close. If you ever want to get your feet wet, let me know. I'm a certified instructor."

"I'll do that," Gleason said, thinking there was no way in hell would that ever happen. "Say, you ever know a detective named Bill Lundy? He was with the Bradenton department. That's up near you, right?"

"Bradenton's across the bay from Tampa. Friend of yours?"

"No, he just helped out my sister one time. She lives in Bradenton."

"Might've heard that name connected with a drug bust. Believe it had something to do with a biker gang. Not sure."

"Well, she's not a biker," Gleason smiled, the hell he'd gone through with that very case having just been refreshed in his memory. "Have a good night."

Driving down Duval Street he saw that Vino's was still open. A couple of vacant chairs waited invitingly on the porch. He pulled over and parked.

This was his favorite spot for people watching. He ordered a glass of merlot and was about to settle in when the phone in his pocket rang.

"Hello," he answered.

"Where the hell are you?" a woman demanded in an angry voice.

"I'm having a glass of wine at Vino's. Where are you?"

A moment of silence and then the line went dead.

Gleason crossed his fingers in the hope that Carl Napier's cheap phone had enough features to capture the caller's number. His wine came.

Chapter 7

Gleason looked up from his desk to see Detective John Cawben holding two cups of coffee.

"Thought you might need one of these," Cawben said. "Looks like you had a late night."

"No, more like an early morning," Gleason said with a yawn and taking one of the cups. "Been here before the chickens got up. You wouldn't happen to have seen this guy around?"

Gleason handed him a print of the suspected murderer.

"Who is he?" Cawben asked.

"According to my witness he's the guy who shot the hearse driver."

"Cold looking bastard. Good drawing, though."

"Yeah, the sketch artist said the witness was pretty specific in describing the jerk," Gleason said. "Patrol has copies but my bet is he's long gone. Miami department also has copies for their watches. Maybe they'll spot him."

"All you can do is keep an eye out and hope you get lucky," Cawben said. "Here's a little trivia for you today about the fentanyl. A lot of the pills found on the street are made in illegal machines bought in China. You can set up shop anywhere. Mexico's a big producer and getting even more so every day, so odds are they came from there. Of course, China makes the stuff as well. It's usually sold by Chinese online pharmacies. Problem is, you don't know what you're getting from either place. Some pretty bad stuff out there. Just a little tidbit to pass on to any of your neighbors who might be in the market."

"I'll keep that in mind," Gleason said. "Yeah, I heard about Mexico being in the game big time. More than ever now since El Chappo is out of the picture. I read that the new outfit that took his place are a bunch of vicious bastards, too. Anyway, this batch we found was a hell of a lot of pills, no matter where they were made. Miami DEA believes a Honduran cartel is involved. Agent there I know there told me that a sizable shipment of cocaine's coming in. I met with him yesterday. Said they were probably going to lace the coke with the fentanyl to make it more addictive. Users would have to keep coming back for more, if you can believe that."

"Oh, I can believe it. So the bad guys were heading back to Miami when the accident happened?"

"Apparently so. The hearse is registered to a Miami mortuary. Supposed to have come here to pick up a body according to the owner of the funeral home. He seemed confused over who was driving the thing. Never heard of our victim. Started to become a 'who's on first' thing. Surprisingly, the DEA agent did recognize the victim's name from an earlier incident. Guess it really is a small world, huh?"

"Seems to be true in the crime business," Cawben said.

"You've got a point there," Gleason nodded, as the mysterious phone call last night ran through his mind.

~~~

Jack's wakeup call came just before sunrise courtesy of the Key West wakeup service. A handsome rooster had recently taken up residence in his backyard with a couple of lady friends. Jack had named him Big Ben.

Another hour or so of sleep would've been great. The Troubled Birds had stopped by the Undrinkable Bar the night before. Angela, Tina and Krysta. They were all from Liverpool, England. And his hunch about the blues influencing their music was right. They knew every blues player that'd ever lived. They had partied until long after closing. He never did learn why Billy originally wanted to talk with him about them. More curiously, was how Billy had met them in the first place? But it hadn't mattered. He had booked the band after hearing them play at the Schooner Wharf Bar.

The auto repair shop had left a message on his phone late yesterday. The Jeep was ready. He'd been futzing around the house all morning waiting for them to open. He was just about to leave when his phone chirped. Caller ID revealed Gleason's name.

"What's up, Earl?" Jack answered.

"How well did you know Carl Napier?"

"Wow, that's a question out of the past," Jack answered. "Carl Napier. Not well at all other than he's a dickhead. He's definitely not a friend of mine."

"But he is a friend of Astrid Kelly, right?"

"Another question from the ages. Frankly, I don't know what their relationship is at the moment. Nor do I care. Why are you asking about those two?"

"I'll get to that. Have you seen either of them lately?"

Jack thought about the sailboat he saw passing Ft. Zach. He wasn't certain it was Astrid's. Should he mention it? He didn't want to look foolish.

"Well, this might sound crazy but I might've seen her boat yesterday, if that counts."

"Where was that?" Gleason asked.

"At the Ft. Zach beach. It was heading east. But again, it might not have been hers. The boat was pretty far offshore. Are you going to tell me what this is all about?"

Gleason paused.

"Carl Napier was the person you saw getting his brains blown out," he stated.

Now it was Jack's turn to pause. This was stunning news.

"You still there, Hunter?" Gleason asked.

"Yeah, just trying to take it in. I mean, I didn't much care for the guy but I wouldn't have wished that on anyone."

"Like you to come to the station and look at a drivers license photo. Confirm it's the same person you knew."

"I'll be there in about twenty minutes."

Gleason ended the call and took a sip of his coffee. It'd grown cold. A uniformed officer entered the detectives room.

"You wanted to see me, detective?" he asked.

"Officer Ed Stone," Gleason smiled, looking up. "Welcome back. Congratulations on being the new tech expert."

"Thanks," Stone said. "Still working patrol, however. What can I do for you?"

"Want you to look at a cellphone. It's a cheap burner and was being used in a homicide I'm investigating. Maybe there's some information in the thing. I didn't want to take a chance with it myself."

Gleason unlocked his desk drawer, took out the phone and gave it to the officer.

"Seems a little more expensive than your usual burner," Stone said, examining the phone. "Whose is it?"

"Homicide victim's."

Right then the cellphone rang.

"What should I do?" Stone said, eyes wide.

"Answer the damn thing!" Gleason hissed. "And put on record, if it has one."

"Hello…" Stone said tentatively into the phone.

Gleason grabbed his own phone and put it on record.

"Carl, is that you?" a female voice spilled into the room.

"Uh…yeah."

"Thank goodness. I've been so worried. You were supposed to be here. Where are you?"

"Accident," Gleason mouthed, then whispered, "Say you had an accident and you're still in Key West. Ask her where she is."

"I…uh…had a little accident," Stone said. "Everything's okay. I'm still in Key West. Where are you?"

"Where we agreed I'd be," the voice replied. "Are you all right, Carl? You sound different."

Detective Sonny Breaks stuck his head in the door of the detectives room.

"Officer Stone," he barked loudly. "When you're finished talking with Detective Gleason there, stick around for a few minutes. I need to ask you something about a case I'm working on. Be right back. Don't go anywhere."

Breaks disappeared and the cellphone connection went dead.

~~~

The airport security guard had been making his last round at the parking garage when he'd noticed the Lincoln Navigator straddling the line between two spaces. The garage wasn't normally on his duty route. He was filling in for another person who was out sick. He'd decided to cut the Navigator's owner some slack. It had a Florida license plate. Probably a local. Maybe the driver was late to make a flight and had been a little careless. The garage wasn't all that full anyway. Flights in and out of the airport were picking up but nowhere near back to normal. Besides he was in a hurry to get home himself. He had couple of days off and he and his wife were driving up the Keys. So he gave the guy a break and went on his way.

But now he was back at work and still assigned to covering the garage. And the Lincoln Navigator was also still there hogging two spaces. Like it was putting it in his face. Well, he'd write him up this time.

He walked over to place the parking ticket under the vehicle's windshield wiper. Glancing inside he noticed that the keys had been left in the ignition switch. A closer look revealed someone sprawled on the rear seat. He tapped on the side window but got no response. He tried the door. It was unlocked. He pulled it open and immediately caught an odoriferous whiff of something dead.

~~~

Jack was waiting at the front desk for Gleason when Sonny Breaks pushed into the room.

"Good morning, Detective Breaks," he greeted.

Breaks brushed past without a word and continued out of the station. Jack noticed the desk officer suppressing a grin. He turned to see Gleason standing in the doorway leading to the back area.

"Follow me, Hunter," he said gruffly.

Jack wondered if Breaks might have had something to do with what was going on but thought better of asking. He followed Gleason to the detectives room.

"I want you to listen to a telephone call I recorded," Gleason said, all business while picking up his cellphone. "Pay special attention to the woman's voice. Never mind the idiot yelling at the end."

He played the message, stopping a little beyond Sonny Breaks' interruption.

"That call was made earlier this morning," Gleason said. "There was also one from the same woman last night. What I'd like to know is do you recognize her voice?"

"Could I hear it again?"

Gleason replayed the message, again cutting off where Breaks entered.

"Once more," Jack asked. "Let it play all the way through this time."

When it had finished, Jack nodded.

"Maybe I wasn't so crazy after all," he said. "That probably was Astrid's boat I saw at Fort Zach."

"Then you recognize the voice?" Gleason asked. "You're saying that it's Astrid Kelly?"

"Sounds like her. I mean, I think so. Not the best recording. Kind of tinny. She was still talking when the other person broke in. I couldn't make out exactly what she was saying. Anyway, that's why I wanted to listen to the whole thing again."

"That's truly amazing, Hunter. I never realized she said anything more after Breaks butted in. Maybe the techs can isolate it from all the other racket."

So that's who the *idiot* was, Jack surmised with a little smile. Breaks must've gotten a world-class chewing out for that. Explains why he left in a big huff.

"You said you wanted me to look at some pictures," he said.

"Two photos, in fact. One from Napier's drivers license and another apparently taken earlier."

He handed Jack the drivers license shot.

"Yes, I'd say that was Carl Napier," Jack said, returning the photo.

"How about this one?" Gleason asked, giving him the booking picture.

"Yep, that's Carl Napier, too. Why do you need me to identify him? You've got enough ID here."

"One of my quirks," Gleason said.

"Where did this second photo come from?" Jack asked. "Just out of curiosity."

"Los Angeles. Booking shot. Napier was arrested there for dealing. Our mutual friend, Detective Laura Dalton, furnished it."

Jack picked up the drivers license photograph again.

"I'm not surprised about Napier dealing," he said. "He used to keep Astrid Kelly supplied with coke."

He compared the two photographs.

"It's strange," he said. "In the booking picture he looks like he did when I first met him. But on the drivers license he's droopy-faced like he was the last time I saw him that night at the restaurant. Different haircut, too. I'd hardly recognized him back then."

"Yeah, I noticed the difference between the facial expressions myself," Gleason agreed. "Maybe he suffered a stroke or something."

"I'd wondered at the time if he'd had plastic surgery," Jack said. "Wound up getting a lousy job. I knew a fellow who had work done around his eyes. Tightened up the skin. Pretty vain about wrinkles. Made him look like an owl."

"I'll ask at the autopsy about the surgery. Although I doubt it'll shine any light on why he was driving that hearse. You wouldn't know if Napier has any family in LA, would you? I need to notify someone about his death and find out what to do with the body. Otherwise, he's headed for a potter's field."

"That's a sad thing to have happened to you at the end," Jack said. "Kind of like you never existed. All I know is he once had some connection there but I couldn't say if it was family or not. Has to be some family somewhere, wouldn't you think?"

"Well, LAPD said they'd look into it. Maybe they'll find out."

"How's Laura doing," Jack asked. "Haven't heard from her in a long time."

"She and her fiancé are taking a time out, whatever that means."

Chapter 8

"I grabbed hold of the door handle, detective, but I was wearing gloves. Carry over from the virus days. Required to wear them then, you know. Yeah, I slammed it shut soon as I saw him and called my supervisor. I understand about not destroying evidence. Sure thing there."

"Thank you, Mr. Pittman. And would you tell me again when you first spotted the vehicle?"

Detective Sam Merrill was talking with Joe Pittman, the airport security officer who'd discovered the body. Merrill had answered the patrol sergeant's call for a detective.

"Sure thing. Three days back it was. I saw it had encroached on the next parking space but I thought I'd give the driver a break and not ticket him. He would've had to pay a fine. Things have been tough enough financially on everybody. Anyway, I came back to work and the car was still there. Well, you know the rest. Have to do what you have to do."

"Is there a security camera in this part of the garage?" Merrill asked, noticing an empty bracket on the wall.

"Was one up there," Pittman said. "It's been down for a couple of weeks. They've put in a work order for a new one, though."

"All right, Mr. Pittman, you can leave," he said. "If we need you for anything else, I'll give you a call."

"Sure thing."

"Here comes the flatbed, detective," a patrol officer announced.

Merrill, disappointed about the missing security camera and the loss of any possible information it might've provided, stood aside as the truck pulled up. The driver got out and Merrill walked over to him.

"I'm Detective Sam Merrill," he said. "What's your name?"

"Willie Baker."

"Well, here's what we have, Willie. For the moment, I'm considering this vehicle a possible crime scene. Wear gloves and don't touch anything more than you have to. When you get it secured on your truck, an officer will cover the vehicle with a tarp. Then, a patrol car will escort you to the impound yard."

"Don't think I can get that SUV pulled up on the bed inside here," Willie said, eyeing the overhead. "Looks a little close. Better if I pull the vehicle out a ways first."

"You're the man, Willie," Merrill said. "Do what's best but try not to shake things up too much."

"Yes, sir, I'll treat it like it's mine," Willie said, glancing apprehensively at the SUV. "I heard something about a dead man being in this thing. Is he still there?"

"Yes."

Merrill had decided to leave the body in situ on the back seat. Though he could see no obvious evidence of foul play, the death was nonetheless suspicious. Particularly in the way the body was positioned on the seat. He thought it would be better to have the vehicle transported, body remaining inside, to the impound where a thorough forensic investigation could be done. He had called the coroner's office and they'd agreed to conduct their examination there. He could look for any identification the dead man carried once the coroner had released the body. He'd taken pictures on his cellphone of the body and the surrounding parking area, although they couldn't be used as evidence. Only photos taken by an official police photographer qualified for that. He just wanted his own to study. The entire floor of the parking garage had been closed at his direction. Finally, the Lincoln Navigator was loaded aboard the flatbed, secured and covered with a plastic tarp. The sad cortege left the airport for the impound. Merrill remained at the parking spot. He always did that. Sometimes you just get a feeling.

~~~

"Detective Gleason, this is Blake Hardy. I've finished the autopsy on Mr. Napier."

Gleason had gone out for lunch and was back at his desk waiting to hear from Officer Stone concerning the recorded telephone message.

"Sorry to have missed the show," he said. "What have you got?"

"I'll run down the list," Hardy said. "Male, age mid-forties…"

"Forty-eight according to his drivers license," Gleason interrupted.

"I'll make a note of that, detective," Hardy replied dryly. "Now, as I was saying, victim appeared healthy, displaced fracture of left thumb, no other injuries, internal organs looked good, stomach contents showed he recently consumed some pizza—probably eaten cold considering the time of morning, I doubt if anything was open—no traces of alcohol, haven't done a drug screen yet. That's about it. Oh, cause of death was a gunshot wound to the head. Other than that, he would've survived the accident."

"I have a question," Gleason said, ignoring the dark humor. "Picture on Napier's drivers license shows a droopiness around one of his eyes and the corner of his mouth sags. Older booking photo doesn't show that. Any thoughts?"

"I'd need to see the pictures before I could give an opinion," Hardy said. "And then it would just be a guess. Unless they were gross, facial features tied to nerve damage wouldn't have been prominent postmortem. But there are a couple of possibilities. He could've been suffering from Bell's Palsy when the license photo was taken. It's a muscle paralysis. Generally, lasts for only a few months, nine at the most. Clears up on its own but there are medicines you can take. Sometimes a brain tumor presents in facial deformation. I didn't examine the brain other than for the extent of injury. How important is this?"

"I honestly don't know if it has any bearing on the case at all," Gleason said. "Just curious."

"Well, another cause for nerve injury leading to facial deformation could have come from getting whacked up side the head, as they say. Or even plastic surgery that didn't turn out as well as hoped, although I'd have thought he was a little young to be having that done. Still, there's no accounting for vanity."

"Can you tell if he'd had plastic surgery done?"

"Let me look at him again. If it was botched, there might be scars."

"I like the whacked-up-side-the-head angle, too."

~~~

"Took a little effort but she's all ready to go," the garage mechanic said, handing Jack the bill. "What's the license plate mean? *DOORSTP.*"

Jack grinned.

"My grandmother had an old conch shell she used for a door stop," he explained. "Gave me the idea for it."

The mechanic gave him a blank look.

"You know…conch shell? Conch? Key West?"

Jack wondered if his vanity plate was that vague or was it just this guy. No one had ever asked him about it before. Maybe he had been too clever. He turned his attention to the repair bill.

"Didn't look like there was this much damage to me," he said. "A few scratches on the grill were all I could see."

"Those weren't deep," the mechanic said. "We rubbed them out. No charge. But you told us to check out everything, so we took you at your word. Don't know when your Jeep was last serviced or what kind of service it has been getting, but the steering was completely shot. Been dangerous to drive much longer left alone. Surprised you hadn't noticed how shaky it was getting. Whole frontend needed rebuilding. New wheel bushings, tie-rod ends, new shocks. Had to replace the steering box with a new one. Can't repair them. Parts for that performance suspension package somebody had put on were a lot more expensive than stock ones, too. Everything's there on the bill."

"So I see," Jack said.

He did remember telling them to look the Jeep over while it was there. However, he didn't recall telling them to run it down the assembly line again. Should've called him first. As far as the last time it was serviced, he couldn't remember that, either. He thanked the man and loaded his bicycle in the Jeep. Before leaving, he wondered again if his vanity plate was too vague.

Cruising at a decent clip along North Roosevelt Boulevard, he had to admit that it drove better. Felt tight. He gave the steering wheel a couple of quick little yanks back and forth. Instant reaction. Like riding on rails, he thought with a grin. A car behind him honked.

He continued driving without further road antics to the post office. All the traffic lights were timed in his favor and he was soon emptying a mail box stuffed full of mostly junk and headed for the recycling bin, except for one letter he held aside. He would wait until he was home to open it.

The parking lot was as far as he got. He climbed into the Jeep and looked at the envelope. There was a different return address. Regimental headquarters in some infantry unit. Also an Army Post Office number in New York. He knew an APO number meant overseas delivery. Removing the letter, he saw it was brief. Handwritten and on a single page. He read it twice.

An old saying his Uncle Leslie often used came to mind. *Irish goodbye.* That was sneaking out of a party without telling anyone. Saved a lot of time and trouble.

He read the letter once more and stuck it back in the envelope. He'd also noticed another difference in the return address. It listed *Major* Rachel Powers. So her promotion had come through. She will do well, he thought, and in truth he was genuinely happy for her if not for himself.

A clucking hen ushering a brood of chicks through the parking lot brought a smile to his face. He started the Jeep's motor and drove away.

Chapter 9

Detective Sam Merrill had supervised getting the Lincoln Navigator off the flatbed at the impound. He'd left the airport garage without gaining anything useful and had driven straight there. Official police photographs had been taken and the coroner's team had completed their examination and removed the body from the vehicle.

"James Rivera," Merrill read aloud from the dead man's drivers license. "Lives in Miami. Make that lived in Miami."

"Okay if we take him?" one from the coroner's team asked.

"Yeah," Merrill said. "There's nothing else on him I need. Appreciate getting an autopsy report soon."

"That's up to the coroner, sir."

"I'll hold on to the victim's billfold," Merrill said. "Have the coroner save that wedding ring and wristwatch he's wearing and all his clothes for evidence, okay?"

"That's routine, sir."

Merrill smiled.

"Of course it is," he apologized. "Sorry. Thanks."

The body bag was zipped closed and loaded into the coroner's van. Forensics started going over the Lincoln and Merrill headed back to the police station.

He'd no sooner sat down at his desk when his phone rang.

"Merrill," he answered.

"Detective, this is Fred Weaver at the impound. Found something interesting on that Lincoln Navigator right after you left and thought you should know. License plate's rigged."

"Say again?"

"Maybe fabricated is a better word. We ran the plate and got no joy. Took a closer look and discovered the plate was made from two separate ones cut in half and the different sides welded together. Professional looking job, too. That's a first for me. My guess is the vehicle's also probably stollen. We're running the VIN number. Forensics still going over the interior. I'll get back to you."

"That's pretty wild about the plates," Merrill said. "Have the print tech go over the whole interior, especially the steering wheel. Maybe the last driver was careless. Oh, here's another thought. Print both license plates front and back. Might find something there."

Gleason entered the detectives room carrying a cup of coffee.

"Sam, what's the story on the airport call?" he said. "I was out of the office when it came in."

"Security guard discovered a DB in a parked car. Coroner has the body, forensics has the car."

"Sounds suspicious," Gleason said, sipping his coffee.

"The car's certainly suspicious. Haven't heard back from the corner yet. "

Gleason grinned and sat down at his desk.

"The security guard had noticed the vehicle earlier," Merrill explained. "Big Lincoln SUV. Sloppy parking job taking up two spaces. He gave the owner a break and didn't ticket it. A few days later he found it was still there, so this time he writes it up and sees the keys are still in the ignition. Looks in the back side window and spots somebody lying on the seat. Turned out he was dead."

"Homicide or what?" Gleason asked.

"I couldn't tell," Merrill said. "Nothing obvious that I could see anyway. Could've been homicide or natural causes. But it was odd, you know? The way the body was positioned. Didn't look like he'd died in his sleep. More like he'd been thrown into the back. Thought it best to treat it as a suspicious death. I decided not to disturb the scene any further so I had the car, with the body left in place where it was, trucked to the impound. Coroner's team made their initial examination there. Didn't find any sign of a wound, either. Maybe I was being too cautious."

Gleason nodded. Or maybe not, he thought. You never know.

"Here's the kicker," Merrill added. "Just got a call from impound that the license plates are not only probably stolen but made up from two separate plates welded together. They're checking the Lincoln's VIN."

"What will they think of next?" Gleason said. "Any ID on the dead guy?"

"Yeah, drivers license. Older dude from Miami. Name's James Rivera. I'll phone Miami PD and ask them to inform any family there."

"Hold off on that for the moment," Gleason said, getting to his feet and dumping the coffee cup into the wastebasket. "Let's go to the airport. I'll fill you in on the way."

~~~

"I told Billy about the Troubled Birds," Derrick Bean said. "He promised to pass it on to you. Guess he kind of got things mixed up."

Jack had driven to Stella-by-Starlight after leaving the post office. Derrick was the chef and a partner in the restaurant. He was considering adding a sushi bar to the restaurant and had called Jack to get his opinion. That and having him sign off on the new stove he'd purchased. During the conversation, Jack had mentioned booking the Troubled Birds for the Undrinkable Bar.

"Mate of mine from England was visiting here a couple of weeks ago," Derrick said. "I was showing him around and we stopped at Schooners. The Troubled Birds were on stage and amazingly he'd heard them playing in some London dive bar. Said they were activists in the immigration troubles over there and decided make it their band's name."

"Well, now they'll be playing in our dive bar," Jack said. "Made the deal myself directly with them. Handle their own gigs. No agent to complicate things. Seems their former agent was a boyfriend of one. Started ripping them off. The other two insisted they dump him. Figured they couldn't do any worse. They just go by their stage names. Keep it simple. I don't even know their last names. They're incorporated, though. Checks go to it."

"Looks and talent are all you need to get anywhere," Derrick laughed. "So what's new with that murder? Billy told me you're the star witness."

"Billy should've kept his mouth shut."

"You know Billy," Derrick laughed again. "Don't tell him anything you don't want to read in the papers the next day."

"It's not funny," Jack said seriously. "I knew the guy who was shot. Wasn't a friend but the police haven't found the person who did it."

"You think he still might be in Key West?" Derrick asked.

"I don't know what the hell to think anymore."

Derrick placed a hand on Jack's shoulder.

"I didn't mean to sound like an ass about Billy," he said. "This has got to be tough on you. Anything I can do to help?"

"Yeah, pretend you don't know me if anyone asks."

~~~

"Mr. Pittman, got a minute?" Merrill called out.

Merrill and Gleason caught Joe Pittman as he was leaving the security office at the airport.

"Sure thing," Pittman said, as the two detectives walked up. "How are you, Detective Merrill?"

"Doing well. This is Detective Gleason. He has a couple of questions about that SUV."

"Sure thing."

"Good to meet you," Gleason said, extending his hand. "I think the vehicle may be involved in a case I'm working on. Maybe we should go back inside your office to talk."

"Sure thing."

The office was furnished with a desk on which sat a tv console, a couple of chairs to the side and a filing cabinet. A large split-screen video monitor hung on the wall facing the desk.

"Bathroom's in there, if anyone needs it," Pittman said, pointing to a door and settling in a chair behind the desk.

"We're fine," Gleason smiled, giving his attention to the video screen which was constantly changing to different locations. "Detective Merrill told me the security camera in the garage where the SUV was parked is missing. Everything seems to be working now."

"The console's programed to switch to the different locations throughout the airport every three minutes," Pittman explained. "Covers ticketing, TSA, waiting area. no cameras in the bathrooms, though, ha, ha."

Gleason gave him a fishy look.

Pittman cleared his throat.

"If a camera goes off line, we take it out of the order." he said. "Here's the area you're talking about,"

Pittman clicked a switch on the console and one section of the screen went dark.

"How about those cameras in other locations around the airport?" Gleason asked, sweeping a hand at the wall. "Any of them been out of the order lately?"

"Nope. Just the one in that area of the garage. New camera should be here any day now. Soon as you free up the garage, we'll get it installed and running."

"Do you record every camera location on tape?" Gleason asked.

Pittman chuckled.

"Tape's so yesteryear, detective. Everything's digital these days. Holds more information and gives a much cleaner picture. Surprised you didn't know that. Each camera is archived for ninety days."

He chuckled again to himself and shook his head. Gleason narrowed his eyes at him.

"I'd be interested in seeing what each of those cameras has recorded during this past week starting with the airport entrance driveway, if the one there is in the order, of course," he said. "Is that possible?"

"Sure thing."

Pittman fiddled with the console and the monitor stopped at the airport entrance ramp.

"You have a particular date in mind, detective?" he asked.

"What was the day you first spotted the SUV?"

"Last Tuesday."

"The incident I'm handling was the day before," Gleason said. "Start with Monday and as soon as it's daylight but before the sun rises. Six o'clock should do it."

"Sure thing."

Pittman turned a knob on the console and a time readout showed 5:45 a.m. A few minutes of nothing passed and suddenly a car drove into the frame. Gleason and Merrill sucked in a quick breath. The tan Honda Accord continued through the scene and the screen was once again empty. Fifteen tedious minutes later a black Lincoln Navigator flashed into view and out of the frame in a blink.

"Stop right there," Gleason ordered. "Go back to where that car came in and freeze it."

A moment later the SUV slowly backed into the screen and stopped at the point it had entered.

"Looks a little fuzzy," Gleason said. "Can you make it clearer?"

"It's blurred because he was going so fast," Pittman explained. "Shouldn't have been driving like that. There's a speed limit posted on the ramp."

"I can make out the license plate, Earl," Merrill said. "That's our car."

"Can't see the driver," Gleason said. "Anyway to blow up the picture?"

"Sure thing."

The car began to expand.

"That's the best I can do, detective."

"There's a damn flare on the windshield," Gleason groaned.

"Looks like a reflection," Merrill said. "I can see a little bit of the driver now. Can't tell if anyone else is in there. Maybe something can be done to make the picture better."

"Good thought," Gleason agreed and turned to Pittman. "I need a copy of this. How soon can I get it?"

"Can't do that without checking first with my supervisor. Don't think he's in today."

"Let me explain the ramifications of what's going on here, sir," Gleason said in his best command voice. "This is a homicide investigation we're conducting. And this tape or digital recording or whatever you want to call it, is now considered to be evidence. I can get a court order to have it released but if I were you and rather than cause any delay, I'd have that copy waiting for me when we return to the station. Am I clear?"

"Sure thing."

Gleason gave him his card and the two detectives left the security office and went to their car.

"Think you were a little short with him back there?" Merrill asked.

"He deserved it."

"Yeah?"

"Sure thing."

~~~

Officer Ed Stone was at the front desk when Gleason and Merrill walked into the police station.

"Detective Gleason," he greeted. "I've got some information on that phone call."

"Great. Come on back and let's hear it."

All three went to Gleason's desk in the detectives room.

"Your friend Jack Hunter was right," Stone said. "There was more conversation after the interruption."

"Someone opened his big mouth while I was recording the call," Gleason explained to Merrill. "I'm not saying who."

Merrill grinned. The word about that was already out.

"So what've you got, Ed?" Gleason asked.

"The cellphone tower triangulation points to the call coming from Miami," Stone said. "Don't have the caller's number. Takes a while to get that from the phone company. As far as what was being said amounted to a couple of choice expletives. I've written them down for you."

He handed Gleason a sheet of paper.

"She certainly has a way with words," Gleason smiled.

"There were some background sounds of a horn blowing," Stone continued. "More likely from a boat than a car. She might've been close to a marina. Crime lab forensics could break it down to specifics but it might take a little more time."

Gleason considered that possibility for a moment. Jack Hunter had mentioned seeing Astrid Kelly's sailboat. Could she have been heading to Miami then?

"Need your opinion on something else," he said. "Got a security camera picture of a vehicle. Has a big flare or reflection on the windshield. Think it could be removed to make out the driver a little better?"

"That's another one for the crime lab in Ft. Myers," Stone said.

"Too bad about not having the caller's number," Merrill said.

"I know someone who might have it," Gleason said.

Gleason thanked Stone and he left.

"Should I continue working on the James Rivera death?" Merrill asked. "If it turns out to be a homicide, that'd go to you, right?"

"They're connected regardless of the cause of deaths so we should work together as partners. You focus on the SUV I'll take the hearse."

"That's terrific," Merrill said. "Do we have to clear that with the Lieutenant?"

"I'll run it by him. He'll be fine."

"If it's okay, I'd like to go to the impound and check on how the forensics are coming."

"See you later," Gleason said.

Chapter 10

Jack had driven to Ruth LaVere's house on Ashe Street where he'd once lived. He parked in front and walked around to the back. The place never failed to dredge up memories.

Derrick Bean lived there now. Ruth, who was presently staying in Swanquarter, North Carolina, with Bobby Sunshine, still owned the property but Jack paid to keep up the maintenance. Derrick's being around contributed to the security.

At one time, Jack had hoped to buy the little house for himself if Ruth were willing to sell. But he'd realized that it also held a history dear to her and never made an offer.

An escaped noise, with no identifiable source and no discernible destination, caught his attention. It seemed to have come from beneath the house.

Suddenly, an iguana the size of an adolescent alligator shot out from the crawlspace and scampered across the backyard to the alley. Jack gave a little yelp and jumped back.

Once he'd recovered his wits, he figured the lizard probably lived in the cemetery. There was a large community of them there. Perhaps it was just visiting. Or it could've found a new home. He preferred not to consider that possibility.

Satisfied that all was right with the house, he left for the Inedible Cafe.

~~~

Sam Merrill's cellphone was on its fifth ring when he finally fished it out from between the car front seats where it'd fallen. It had slipped from his hand when he pulled it from his pocket. He should get a holder for the thing, he thought.

"This is Merrill," he said, switching it to speaker rather than pulling over and stopping. He was in a hurry to get to the impound.

"Detective Merrill, sorry if I've awakened you. This is Blake Hardy at the coroner's office."

"My phone was temporarily out of touch," Merrill said.

"That can be a blessing at times. I have a cause-of-death on the gentleman you sent us. Old fashioned heart attack."

"So it was a natural death after all," Merrill said, somewhat surprised. "I wasn't sure. At the scene he didn't look like he'd died in his sleep."

"Well, this is just a preliminary finding," Hardy said. "I'll do a complete workup. But the heart was in pretty bad shape. A coronary in waiting. There is something else, however, I thought you should know, which is why I'm calling now. A large tuft of his hair had been yanked out. Also, his chest showed a deep scratch most likely from a fingernail and his shirt was ripped."

"Like someone roughed him up?" Merrill asked.

"No, the injuries were postmortem. You said something about the body's position?"

"Yeah, like he hadn't snuggled down for a nap. More like sprawled halfway on the backseat. That's why I considered it suspicious. Possibly there'd been a struggle of some kind and he had gotten the worst of it."

"If so, he was already dead when it took place."

~~~

"It was Derrick who wanted the new stove for Stella-by-Starlight, Billy. You told me you needed one here."

Jack and Billy were in the kitchen at the Inedible Cafe.

"Don't remember saying that," Billy frowned.

56

"Doesn't matter," Jack smiled. "It's all settled. By the way, I noticed that Derrick has a houseguest. Rather an under-the-house guest."

"You must be talking about ol' Iggy, hee-hee."

"Iggy?" Jack laughed. "He named that thing? How long has it been there?"

"For some time now. Comes out when Derrick calls him, too. Iggy knows he's going to have flowers for dinner. You see, Derrick brings home the old flowers that decorate the tables at the restaurant when they replace them. Not that they're dried out or anything, Derrick just likes a fresh look. Doubt if Iggy can tell the difference. Old flowers probably just as tasty as new ones to him, hee, hee."

Jack made a face.

"But why would Derrick ever even want something like that living under the house?" he asked.

"Because nothing else gonna come snooping around while Iggy's there."

"Didn't know there was a problem with…uh, snoopers."

"There ain't anymore, hee-hee."

"Whatever works," Jack said. "Troubled Birds playing tonight?"

"Tomorrow night. Those ladies got real talent, Jack. You should join in with your saxophone."

"They'd blow me off the stage."

"One of them thinks you're cute, hee-hee."

Jack shot Billy a sideways glance.

"Well, I think they're all great," he said. "Cute, too. Here's something funny. Thought I saw Astrid Kelly's sailboat the other day. Passing off Ft. Zach. Pretty wild, huh?"

Billy didn't comment.

"Wasn't completely sure but it definitely looked like her boat," Jack continued. "Another thing that isn't so funny is the guy I saw shot was a friend of Astrid's. They were both here that night of my birthday with another couple from Miami. Big drug traffickers. Now somehow it looks like Astrid could be back in the picture again."

Jack decided not to tell Billy about the telephone call Gleason had recorded. No question that it'd been Astrid on the line. He'd recognized her voice immediately but had been a little coy in coming right out and saying so. He'd thought about that hesitancy afterwards but couldn't find any reason for his behavior. Perhaps there was nothing to it.

"Best you keep away from her," Billy warned sternly. "Miss Astrid's a nightmare woman."

"She couldn't be farther from my mind," Jack shrugged.

"What's the latest on the lady soldier friend of yours?" Billy asked in a lighter tone.

"She got a big promotion."

"I knew she was going places," Billy said proudly.

Chapter 11

"The SUV was reported stolen two months ago in Hialeah, detective," Fred Weaver said. "Miami police suspect a car theft ring they've been trying to catch. Take orders for specific models. Usually those vehicles are shipped out of the country for overseas customers but this baby stayed in town."

"Maybe it missed the boat on purpose," Merrill said. "Could've been a local order. What I'm interested in right now is human hair. Specifically, a large hank. You find anything like that?"

"As a matter of fact, we did. On the floor in the back. Thought it might've come from a dog that was shedding. We bagged it separately before vacuuming the whole interior for trace evidence. Think it belonged to the victim?"

"The coroner mentioned the possibility. DNA testing would confirm that providing there's enough follicle on the strands, although I understand now they can possibly get it from just the hair. This thing's becoming more like trying to put together a jigsaw puzzle in the dark. What about the license plate? Any prints on it?"

"Nope. Good idea, though."

"Well, thanks, Fred. I better get back to the station."

"Wait a minute," Weaver said. "One more thing. We found a slug under the passenger seat in the hearse. Slightly deformed but possibly enough of the grooves left to ID. The crime lab can also do a metallurgical analysis to find a match. We bagged it and are sending it over. Pass that on to Detective Gleason, will you?"

Gleason was still at his desk when Merrill arrived.

"The security camera footage came in right after you left," he said. "Ft. Meyers has a copy now."

"I was wondering if we should've taken the camera and all," Merrill said. "What do you think?"

"I asked the technician at the crime lab about that. Her name's Anne Nilsson. We've worked with her before. Good person. She said the copy would be okay. If it turns out they do need the camera, we'll get an court order."

"Before I forget," Merrill said, "forensics found a slug in the hearse. They're sending it over. Also, the coroner at the body shop called while I was on the way to the impound. Rivera died from a heart attack."

"The body shop?"

"Sorry," Merrill said. "That's what we called the morgue in Tampa. Anyway, Doctor Hardy confirmed it was natural causes."

"And here I thought it couldn't get any better," Gleason said.

"It gets even better. Or worse. Rivera was dead before he got in the back seat. Heart attack. There were postmortem injuries. Hank of hair pulled out. Scratches. He probably kicked off sitting up front and whoever put him there was pretty rough getting him over the seat."

"I just don't understand this whole..." Gleason said, "ahh... here's one possibility, not that it puts us any closer. Jack Hunter said someone was blowing the horn in the SUV. Could've been Rivera needing help."

"Makes sense, I guess," Merrill said.

"Hunter had tentatively identified the mystery caller on the cellphone, too. Astrid Kelly. She was an old flame of his. I'm thinking maybe he still has her phone number."

"You're saying they were involved?" Merrill grinned. "Hunter and this Astrid woman. Romantically?"

Gleason chuckled.

"I don't know if there was any hot and heavy romance going on," he said. "Probably was in his mind. But they were acquainted. In fact, he once introduced me to her."

Gleason recounted the Grubber connection and the DEA's involvement at the time.

"This Jack Hunter sounds like an interesting character," Merrill said. "How well do you really know him?"

"Well enough to know the guy's not a crook or a killer if that's what you're getting at. He just has an affinity for finding trouble."

"Troublemaker?"

Gleason laughed.

"No, trouble considers him a kindred spirit and drops by to say hello occasionally."

"But you do trust him?"

"Yeah, I'd have to say that I do," Gleason admitted almost wistfully. "He once saved my butt. That's another story but back to what you were saying about Rivera. He could've been in the rear seat all along. Leaned over the front for some reason and his heart gave out. Died on the spot and fell against the horn. Shooter was in a big hurry to get away, grabbed him up and shoved him back over the seat."

"Yeah, that would explain the injuries," Merrill agreed. "It looked like he'd been heaved into the back. But why was he sitting there instead of riding in front?"

"Maybe he was too sick and had to lie down," Gleason said. "He was the mortuary's regular driver. His boss said he was worried about his health. So Rivera starts having trouble with his heart when they arrive in Key West. Gets worse and he can't drive. Napier takes his place."

"So Napier was in on the drugs?"

"Had to have been," Gleason said. "He was no stranger to dealing. Priors in LA. Hunter said he had drug sources here, too."

"What about the funeral home people?" Merrill asked

"I'm more than a little suspicious about the guy who owns the place. Miami DEA might be, too."

"So who is the shooter then?"

"Could belong to the cartel behind all this drug business. Maybe another Honduran since the main man is from there. His job was to protect the shipment. Things started going south when Rivera crapped out and then it really hit the fan with the accident."

Merrill mulled that over for a moment.

"What baffles me is why your friend Jack Hunter wasn't also shot," he said. "It was pretty coldhearted the way this guy blasted that driver. You have to admit it's odd he'd let Hunter off. I don't know. Makes me wonder if he's involved, too. He knew the victim. Pretty wild coincidence there."

"I think it was blind luck that he survived," Gleason said. "Hunter has always had that going for him. DEA agent told me that the drug syndicates prefer to just kill their own these days but I'm not sure I go along with that. Anyway, Hunter said the car horn seemed to have distracted the shooter. I can see why you would find that hard to believe, though. I wouldn't myself if it were anyone else but him. The sergeant who called me to the scene thought it was road rage. Figured Hunter threw the weapon overboard."

"Sounds reasonable."

"He wanted to get a police diver to look for it," Gleason added. "I told him to save the resources. Lieutenant's already going bonkers over the department budget."

"Not a problem," Merrill smiled. "I'll be the diver. No resources spent."

"I don't believe there's any gun out there," Gleason said, "but if you want to go look for one, at least it'll put that idea to bed."

"Low tide's around seven tomorrow morning," Merrill said. "Meet you there at six-thirty?"

"Fine," Gleason said, turning off his computer. "I'm calling it a day for now."

~~~

Duval Street stretches a mile and a quarter from sea to shining sea. In deference to his broken metatarsal that seemingly defied healing, Gleason had recently taken to nightly walks along the street between both bodies of water, dreams of competing in the Seven

Mile Bridge run having been put on hold. His routine followed a leisurely stroll uptown to the Atlantic Ocean then downtown to the Gulf of Mexico and back up again about midway to Vino's where he would relax in a chair on the porch with a glass or two of merlot.

The walks provided not only a good source of exercise but also an uninterrupted time for thinking. Having settled in a favorite chair and ordered his wine, he reviewed once more where they stood in the Napier homicide. Somewhere lost at sea, he concluded.

Jack Hunter wasn't involved other than having the misfortune of being the sole witness. Sam Merrill may believe otherwise and he'd entertain the detective's idea for tomorrow. James Rivera's role could've been innocent but his boss, Jules Flores in Miami, knows something. Which brings up Astrid Kelly. He really needed to talk with her.

His wine came and before he could take the first sip someone called up from the sidewalk.

"Good evening, Detective Gleason," Jack said cheerfully. "Mind if I join you?"

"What an amazing coincidence," Gleason said. "I was just thinking of you. Come on up. Appreciate your help with something."

Chapter 12

"It was like glass out there yesterday," Merrill said disappointedly. "Absolutely beautiful. I drove by here after you left. Now you could practically surf."

"That going to be a problem?" Gleason asked.

The two men stood on the sidewalk across from the airport surveying the choppy water. A tropical depression lagging off the Yucatan Peninsula while deciding where to move next had kicked up the wind during the night and was now blowing at a steady 20 mph.

"Don't know," Merrill said. "Could affect visibility in the shallower parts."

"Guess it depends then on how good Hunter's arm is," Gleason said.

Merrill bent down and picked up a rock.

"This has about the heft of a Smith and Wesson," he said.

He hurled the rock out over the water. It disappeared in a splash about a hundred feet from shore.

"Good peg," Gleason said. "Could've been a pro."

"I'll start just a little beyond there and work my way back, "Merrill said. "Like walking a lane search. Keep the courses three or four feet apart."

Gleason nodded in agreement.

"When you mentioned diving, I thought you were talking about real gear like you see on a treasure hunt," he grinned. "Wetsuit and air tanks, all that stuff. But just a bathing suit?"

Merrill was dressed in a pair of swim trunks and a yellow t-shirt which matched the yellow flippers on his feet.

"Snorkel's all you need for this job," he said, pulling down his face mask and flip-flopping to the water's edge.

Gleason watched as he swam out toward the spot where the rock had entered.

"This look about where the rock hit?" Merrill yelled, stopping and treading water.

"Best I can tell," Gleason yelled back.

Merrill gave a thumbs-up and began a slow breaststroke to the east, paralleling the road. Only his snorkel was visible from shore. He continued for fifty feet or so, and returned in the opposite direction for approximately the same distance past the starting point. Then again, this time an imperceptible few feet closer in. And so it went for the next hour.

To Gleason it was like watching paint dry. His mind drifted to the night before and his conversation on the porch at Vino's with Jack Hunter. His hunch had been right. Hunter did indeed have Astrid Kelly's phone number stored in his steel-encased cellphone, a similar one having once saved his life by stopping a bullet. And he had willingly given him the number. Now he just had to figure out just how best to use it.

At last, Merrill had finished the search. He'd sloshed along the shoreline in knee-deep water for the last two courses.

"Man, I must've covered a quarter-mile of ocean," he said, toweling off.

"Find anything interesting?" Gleason asked.

"Yeah, what's left of an old outboard motor that's probably been there forever. Bottles, unrecognizable objects and junk, lengths of old rope, people don't give a shit about polluting the ocean."

"No gun, though?"

"Unless your friend has a better arm than mine, no."

Gleason checked his watch.

"See you at the office," he said.

Gleason got in his car and swung an illegal u-turn across South Roosevelt Blvd. He drove on to White Street and stopped at Sandy's Cafe to pick up a sandwich and a Cuban coffee before heading to the police station.

He'd no sooner settled at his desk when Officer Ed Stone popped in.

"Detective Gleason," he said. "Got an ID on that Miami caller. It's a cellphone number"

Stone handed him a copy of an email the telephone company had sent. Gleason compared the phone number on it with the one Jack had given him. They didn't match.

"Something's screwy here," Gleason said.

He pulled out Carl Napier's cellphone from his pocket. He'd been carrying it around in the hope that the woman might call back. She hadn't.

"Let's try something, Ed," he said, handing him the phone. "You've spoken with this person before. Give her a call on that number you have."

"What do I say if she answers?"

"Try 'H-e-l-l-o Astrid'," Gleason said dreamily.

Ed Stone punched in the numbers.

"Not getting anything," he said. "Could be it's blocked but usually you'd first hear a short ring and then nothing. This is weird. I'll hang up and try again."

"Turn the thing off and then back on," Gleason suggested. "Like a reboot."

Stone flicked the phone off and waited a moment before turning it on again. He redialed only to get the same results.

"Nope," he said. "Could be in an area where there's no signal."

The bottom of the ocean crossed Gleason's mind as a possibility.

"You could be right" he said. "I'll hold on to the cellphone. Maybe she'll get lonely and call."

Stone left and Gleason considered another possibility. Suppose it wasn't Astrid Kelly who'd called? Hadn't Jack Hunter been unsure of the voice after listening to the recording? A woman's voice, yes, but someone else, either working with Napier or just a friend. It was entirely possible. And more reason to believe that that particular phone had been tossed. Which further pointed to it having been used as a burner and made finding its owner even more pertinent.

And another thing, how recent was the phone number of Astrid Kelly that Hunter gave him? The idiosyncrasy of Hunter's keeping the phone number of every person he's ever known in his life was fortunate but maybe that one had been changed.

Two different cellphones allegedly belonging to one person. Two different identification photos of one victim. Even two different suspects were under consideration at one time. And Sam Merrill had said something about wild coincidences?

He sipped his cup of Cuban coffee. It'd grown cold.

~~~

Jack stood on the boardwalk at the Key West Bight watching the Party Cat pull out of its berth with a boatload of excited tourists headed for a day on the water. He liked that. The Cat had been docked for a stint during the virus but now it was back in business. The wind had begun to stiffen so they'd better keep to the lee side of the islands unless everyone has a strong stomach, he thought. He was happy to have his feet on solid ground. Or wooden planks, as it were.

He had been nosing around the Bight since early morning. He'd always loved being here at this time of day. It was hustle-bustle time as everything got underway. One of the better shows in town. Even the gulls and pelicans got in the act.

He could've phoned the harbor master for what he'd wanted to know. But he had preferred to do it in person. Sort of mixing business with pleasure.

The question had been knocking around in the back of his mind since he saw the boat passing Fort Zach beach. And his talk with

Gleason last night had added even greater importance to the matter and had pushed him into getting an answer.

He had hoped to learn if the *Justice* had been moored in the harbor at any time during the past couple of weeks.

Gleason had explained to him why it was necessary that they get in touch with Astrid Kelly. She was a friend of Carl Napier, who was in possession of drugs more dangerous than he could imagine. There was reason to believe the drugs belonged to a Honduran cartel. She knew the man running that ring. She had called Napier from Miami. The cellphone she'd used was a burner and no longer existed. This was a very big deal and a lot was at stake. The message had gotten through.

Of course, he'd been fairly sure of what he'd find. The harbor master's records indicated that the *Justice* had tied up there the day before the accident and had sailed the day after.

That had pretty much confirmed Astrid's involvement in the drug scheme. Strangely, it had also disappointed him. Astrid was a lot of things but he'd never figured her for this.

Billy had called her a nightmare woman. A shrink might better put her as a narcissuses. Even a sociopath. Everything was certainly all about her. Fun and exciting to be with as long as things went her way. Then watch out. She used people. Toyed with them to get what she wanted. Could drop you on a whim. A person lacking a conscience. Are you born that way?

She'd used him until he had finally woken up. Used Carl Napier, who for some reason had stuck around regardless of how she treated him. Like a sick puppy. And look where he was now. Headed for an unmarked grave.

The Party Cat reached the channel and plunged on through the chop toward the open water. Jack took a last look at the rows of expensive yachts with seemingly not a living soul aboard any of them and decided to shove off himself.

Chapter 13

The body was sprawled face down across a narrow strip of matted grass running between the street and sidewalk along 13th Avenue in Liberty City. A small group of people had gathered in front of a house on the other side of the street. Patrol cars blocked traffic access at both ends of the block.

"Saw him laying out there this morning," the man said.

"And your name, sir?" Nate Ellis asked.

Ellis was a sergeant with the Miami Police Department and worked in the South District which included the historical black community of Liberty City. He'd been called to the scene by patrol and was questioning the person who'd reported the incident.

"Jamal Rice. That's where I live."

Rice pointed to the modest house behind them.

"I was getting ready to leave for work," he continued. "Went out to see if I could help him. He wasn't moving so I shook him and saw that blood on his shirt. Man, I came right back inside to call the police."

"Did you hear anything last night? Disturbance? Gun shots?"

"Gun shots wouldn't be nothing new around here, officer," Rice said. "But no, didn't hear any shots last night but then I'm a pretty heavy sleeper."

"All right," Ellis said. "The detective will have some more questions when he arrives. Need for you to stick around until he gets here."

"Hope that's soon," Rice said worriedly. "Already called my boss and told him I'm going to be late. He's not going to want to hear it a second time."

The detective showed up shortly. She was an attractive petite woman with close-cropped hair dyed ash-blonde and dressed in a smart black pantsuit. A patrol officer pointed out to where Ellis stood with Rice.

"Good morning, sergeant," she greeted. "I'm Detective Keisha Quorck. What do we have?"

"Good morning to you, detective," Ellis said, surprised but quickly recovering. "Apparent shooting victim. This gentleman discovered the body this morning. Said he didn't hear or see anything last night."

"And your name is, sir?" Quorck asked, turning to Rice.

"Jamal Rice, ma'am. Told the officer here I saw him laying out on the sidewalk when I was about to leave for work this morning and went to see if he was okay. Thought maybe he'd passed out or something."

"Did you try to wake him up, touch him or anything?"

"Yes, ma'am, I tried to wake him and shook him a little. Then I saw the blood and ran straight back inside and called 911. Came back out here in the yard and waited for the police car."

"And you heard nothing last night?" Quorck asked.

"Like I told the officer, I'm a heavy sleeper," Rice said.

Quorck decided there was nothing more Rice could tell her. She thanked him and said she'd call him later if necessary. She turned her attention to the victim.

"He's not from the neighborhood," she said.

"No one we've spoken with so far seems to know him," Ellis said. "We haven't done a house-to-house yet. Could live in another block."

Quorck tightened her mouth.

"What about those parked cars?" she asked, gesturing at the street. "They all local? Maybe one of them belongs to him. Check their registrations."

"I'll have patrol get the plate numbers."

Quorck bent down for a closer look at the body. She took out her cellphone and grabbed a few photos.

"His watch is missing," she said, pointing to the dead man's left wrist. "See there? Strap mark on the skin. Much lighter than the rest of him. Bet he never takes it off."

"Could've been a robbery that went wrong," the sergeant suggested. "Guy resisted. Paid a price."

"Hmm…" Quorck murmured, her attention still on the dead man.

"Haven't checked him for a wallet," Ellis said. "Maybe that was also stolen."

"Hmm.." Quorck murmured again. "We'll wait for the coroner to tell us it's okay to move him. Then we can have a look. But what was he doing here? I don't see him making a street deal. Doubt if he was a crackhead. Too healthy looking. Well, aside from being dead. Then there's that suit he's wearing. Probably had it tailor-made. No, you wouldn't find his type hanging around in this neighborhood. Believe me, I know."

Ellis gave her a puzzled look.

"I grew up the next two blocks over from here, sergeant," she said. "This is my `hood.'"

She smoothed back the front of her pants and looked around at the scene.

"Find any shell casings?" she asked nonchalantly.

"Nothing, detective. Could've been a revolver. Wouldn't have ejected the casing."

"They only use six-shooters in oaters, sergeant," she smiled. "Didn't you know that?"

"Sorry?"

"Just fooling with you. I'm a big western movie fan. They're called oaters because cowboys ride horses and feed them oats and they refer to their guns as six-shooters because they hold six bullets."

"No kidding? You like cowboy movies?"

"It's true. I confess. Mainly, the old ones starring heroes like Gene Autry, Roy Rogers…you name 'em, I know 'em. But don't get me started or we'll never finish here. Anyway, take another look for a casing. Could be hidden in the grass along the street. Flew into someone's yard. Endless possibilities. There's a single bullet wound in his chest and what appears to be powder burns on the shirt. Hardly any blood on the ground. Possible that he was shot elsewhere and dumped here. I've seen enough of the body. You can call the coroner. I'm going across the street to talk with some of those people standing there."

"Aren't you new to us, Detective Quorck?" Ellis asked. "Don't think I've seen you around the station before."

"I'm on loan to South District. Normally I work downtown in Central. Seems your district's shorthanded at the moment so they pulled me in. Temporary duty."

"Yeah, there've been a few retirements lately," Ellis said. "I'll get an officer and we'll look for that casing."

~~~

Sam Merrill walked into the detectives room just as Gleason was getting off the phone with the crime lab in Ft. Myers. The call had been disappointing.

"No joy on that security camera shot," Gleason said. "Couldn't do much with the windshield reflection. Sending us what they have. I didn't ask whether or not they could tell if anyone else was in the car."

"Maybe it will be enough to match the artist's sketch," Merrill said hopefully.

Gleason shrugged.

"What pisses me off is Jules Flores being up to his ass in this mess and I can't do anything about it," he grumbled.

"Guess he now belongs to the DEA since there were drugs."

"But the whole thing started here," Gleason protested. "We deserve to get in a few licks. I'd like to jack up Flores some more. See what happens."

"He'd only cry police harassment," Merrill said. "Probably be right, too. By the way, Miami PD said they'd notify Rivera's family. Kind of ironic that he'll be riding back there in a hearse."

Gleason didn't reply and instead reached for his phone and punched in a number.

"Christo Mortuary," a man answered. "This is Don Gray. How may I help you?"

"My name is Detective Earl Gleason. I'm with the Key West Police Department. I'd like to speak with Jules Flores, please."

"Mr. Flores isn't in at the moment, sir."

Here we go again, Gleason thought to himself.

"Do you have any idea when he will be back?" he asked. "It's important."

"No, sir, I can leave him a message."

"That won't be necessary," Gleason said. "I'll call later. What's your name again?"

"Don Gray. I'm filling in from the temp agency."

"How about Carrie Talick?" Gleason asked. "Could I speak with her?"

"I'm sorry. I don't know of anyone here with that name. She works for the mortuary?"

Now Gleason knew who had been let go in the so-called job consolidation. He wondered who else there had gotten the axe? And why?

"She used to work there," Gleason said. "Tell Flores I'll call later."

He ended the call and looked at the notepad he'd doodled on while talking.

"Kind of interesting drawings," Merrill observed.

"Old habit of mine," he said, tearing off the page and putting it in his desk drawer. "Been doing it a long time. Maybe someday I'll make a book of them."

How many times had he said that, he wondered. Still, maybe someday.

Chapter 14

Jack had played through the entire book of twenty-seven rhythmical exercises on his saxophone and had ended the demanding practice session improvising a bluesy version of *Over the Rainbow.*

He'd done the musical workout hoping it would help clear his head. His morning at the Key West Bight had left him with more on his mind than he'd brought there. To think of the cosmic odds it must have taken to involve him in this whole insane happening. It was overwhelming.

He put away the horn, grabbed the Jeep's keys and set off for the Inedible Cafe. Billy was sweeping the sidewalk in front when he pulled up.

Jack waved a hello and went straight inside to the bar. He rattled out two bottles of beer from the cooler and sat down on a stool. Billy joined him a minute or so later.

"How you been doing, Jack?" Billy asked, eyeing him with some concern. "Things coming along okay?"

"I guess so, Billy. Police are done with Carl Napier. At least that's one thing out of the way. He'll be buried in a potter's field unless they can find a relative to claim him. Not that he was a friend but I think it's kind of sad for anyone to wind up a nobody in a nowhere place."

"I once knew a fellow who was buried at sea," Billy said.

"Sounds about as anonymous," Jack said.

"Had the service at the church, of course," Billy continued. "T. K. Howard preached the sermon and for once kept it short.

Afterwards, they took the poor man down to the bight and laid him on the deck of an old wooden two-masted schooner. All nicely wrapped up and weighted down so he'd sink fast. We got on board and sailed three miles out in the ocean to where it was deep enough to drop him off. Hardly made a splash."

Billy stopped talking to take a long pull from his bottle.

"Now, this fella you're worrying so much about being put in the potter's field all alone and where nobody knows he's at," he said. "Maybe we can fix up something special for him. You tell the police you found out that he's your distant cousin. They turn him over to you because now they have a relative, see? They're off the hook. Next night we fit him up with a couple of window sash weights and Sparrow Lovewell takes all of us out past the reef in his boat. You say a few words and we give your new cousin a proper sendoff. How's that sound?"

Jack had been quietly staring at the floor the whole time. He turned toward Billy and couldn't help but laugh.

"You know, I think we better just let the police handle it," he said.

~~~

Detective Keisha Quorck sat at a borrowed desk in the detectives room at South District. She'd just finished writing the report on the Liberty City homicide. They'd found no wallet on the victim but had discovered a keyring in his pants pocket. It held only a single key which had a star logo. And on the keyring itself was an identification tag listing a telephone number.

She called it now.

"Christo Mortuary," a man answered. "This is Don Gray. How may I help you?"

A mortuary, how perfect, Quorck thought with a wry smile.

"My name is Detective Keisha Quorck. I'm with the Miami Police Department. We're looking into a situation that may involve your company. Is there someone I could speak with about this?"

"That would be Mr. Jules Flores," Gray said. "He's the owner but he isn't in presently. Funny, you're the second detective to call him today."

"My goodness," Quorck said in surprise, a tinge of excitement running through her. "Who was the first?"

"I wrote down his name somewhere," Gray said, rustling through some papers. "Here it is. Detective Earl Gleason. Said he was with the Key West police department."

Quorck thought two detectives from separate jurisdictions calling the same individual had to be more than a coincidence. She jotted down Gleason's name on a notepad.

"Probably selling tickets to the policemen's ball," she said casually.

"Ma'am?"

"My feeble sense of humor," she said. "Pay no attention to it. This other detective, he didn't say what the call was about, did he?"

"No, he just said he would call back."

She toyed with the key in her fingers. Though she wasn't a car buff, she believed it could belong to a Mercedes.

"Would you happen to know what make of car Mr. Flores has?" she asked. "I'm aware that's an odd question but do you know? I'm trying to get something straightened out here."

"Honestly, I have no idea," Gray said. "I'm subbing at this job. Don't work here regularly. I did see a car parked in the back of the mortuary's driveway. Could be his. I doubt if anyone else would be allowed to park there."

Quorck perked up at that.

"Do you remember what make it was?" she asked.

"Just a car is all I remember. Sorry."

"That's all right. How does Mr. Flores spell his name? And what is your address there? Just in case I need to drop by later."

She wrote down the information and hung up. She then immediately put in a request to motor vehicles for Jules Flores' drivers license. She realized that without being specific there could be several Jules Flores in the Miami area. She could wait until she had more information but she'd just sort them out herself. It was also entirely possible that Flores wasn't involved. The dead man was someone else who'd found the key or whatever. But she wouldn't bet on that.

And as for Detective Earl Gleason, she would have to get in touch with him later. Right now it was urgent that she pay a visit to the Christo Mortuary.

Surprisingly, it turned out to be a short drive. The mortuary was a single story white stuccoed structure of ordinary design with a front entrance and neatly trimmed foliage. A covered driveway ran down one side of the building.

Quorck pulled into a vacant space a block past. Walking back to the mortuary she noticed a silver sedan parked at the rear of its drive.

She entered into a lobby with an alcove that apparently served as a reception office and where a young man in his early twenties sat at a small desk.

"Hello, ma'am," he greeted. "May I help you?"

"You must be Don Gray," she said pleasantly, recognizing his voice. "I'm Detective Keisha Quorck."

Gray looked surprised. Quorck had found that to be the usual reaction whenever she introduced herself as a cop. She considered it an edge.

"I saw the car in your driveway," she continued. "Find out anything more about it'?"

"Yes, it's a Mercedes and belongs to Mr. Flores. I asked around after you called."

"Sounds like you should be in my line of work."

Gray gave an embarrassed little laugh.

"I majored in business at college," he said. "Things have been slow to pick up since graduating what with the pandemic and all. This temp job I got from the agency is the best I can do for now."

"Well, the police business is never slow. Might want to consider putting in an application. Like that other outfit says, we're looking for a few good men. Oh, and as many good women as we can get. Could you take me out to where the car's parked?"

Gray led her to the back of the driveway.

"Was the car involved in an accident?" he asked.

"No, just need to confirm something," Quorck smiled.

She slipped on a pair of gloves and checked the driver's door. It was locked. She took out the keyring they'd found on the victim from her purse, presses the remote and opened the door. Leaning in, she pulled down the sun visor to see if the registration was pinned to it. That would have the owner's address. Nothing. She reached across to check the glove compartment. It held only a road map of Florida. She unfolded the map but found no registration that might've slipped inside. Notations were written on the map at several locations throughout the state. The inset for Miami had a number of similar markings. She couldn't make out what they meant. She refolded the map and started to stick it back in the glovebox. Then on second thought, she decided to hold on to it.

"If anyone asks, this car is off limits," she said, shutting the door and locking it. "No one touches it but me."

"I don't understand," Gray said, puzzled. "Why do you have the keys?"

"Can't get into that right now," Quorck answered. "It'd be a big help, however, if I had Mr. Flores' home address and telephone number. Would they be available?"

Gray hesitated before answering.

"Not sure I ought to give that out, ma'am," he said. "Maybe you should wait until Mr. Flores is back and can talk with you. I really don't want to get into trouble."

Quorck knew he didn't have to comply. Confidentiality laws were specific. She also knew not to threaten getting a court order for them. That'd shut down all hope of her walking away with anything more.

"Well, I understand and I certainly don't want you to do anything you'd feel uncomfortable about," Quorck said. "And I definitely don't want you to get into trouble. Just having them might help point me in the right direction so I wouldn't have to waste more time and bother. Anyway, thank you and good luck with getting on with your career."

She took out a business card and handed it to him.

"Call me if you think of anything else. And I meant that about being a cop. Give it some thought."

Gray read the card and put it in his billfold.

"There's an employee phone list in the desk," he said quietly. "Not that there are all that many employees here. Probably old but it might have addresses."

Quorck smiled and followed him back to the office.

Chapter 15

"Looks like it could be a 40 caliber," Gleason said, examining the lead slug before placing it back in the envelope. "I'll have this signed into evidence and then get it off to ballistics at the crime lab. After that, you might want to take another swim in the ocean to see if there's a gun out there that fits it."

Merrill didn't comment. He was studying his computer screen.

"This photo of the SUV's windshield the crime lab sent shows some detail of the driver," he said. "I admit it's not much but it does kind of resemble the sketch. Take another look."

Gleason compared the artist's drawing with the same image on his screen.

"Vaguely," he said. "That is if you squint hard and use a lot of imagination."

"It'd be neat to superimpose them," Merrill said. "You know, put them one over the other. Like they make in movie effects. Camera does a closeup on someone's face and it morphs into different one. I bet if you did that with the security picture and the sketch they'd match up pretty close. Might be more realistic, too."

Gleason thought that over.

"Let me call my friend in the crime lab and run it past her," he said. "You want to go grab us a couple of cups of coffee?"

Merrill returned just as Gleason was finishing up his conversation with the crime lab.

"The slug in the vehicle looks to be the same caliber as the casing we found at the scene," he said. "Thanks."

"What's up?" Merrill asked.

"They like your idea of superimposing the images. Even willing to take another shot at enhancing the windshield photo just for the hell of it. There're already programs that can do that sort of thing. Sending them a copy of the sketch. I mentioned the slug to them since we were talking. Said they can store a digital picture of it and the casing. Be useful to have if the gun it came from has a history."

Gleason's phone rang.

"Gleason," he answered.

"This is the desk, Detective Gleason. You have a call from a detective in Miami. Want me transfer it back to you?"

"Does he have a name?" Gleason asked. "Never mind, yeah, I'll take it."

A moment's silence.

"Hello?" a woman said. "Is this Detective Gleason?

After leaving the Cristo Mortuary, Detective Keisha Quorck had driven past the apartment building listed in the employee directory as Jules Flores' address. It was near the Vizcaya Museum. Built during the construction boom in the late nineties and early 2000s and completed just in time for the real estate crash, the apartments went begging then. It was a few years before things started to pick up. It'd impressed her as a pricey place to live today. She'd decided to stop by later and had now returned to the station.

The information she'd requested from the DMV had been waiting in her computer. There were four Jules Flores registered drivers in the entire state. Number three had matched the address she'd driven past. More to the point, the picture on the license matched the one she'd taken of the victim.

"This is Detective Earl Gleason. May I ask who you are?"

"I'm Detective Keisha Quorck at Miami South District. Your name has come up in a homicide I'm working. Call me back and we can talk."

This was a standard procedure most police departments followed to confirm identity. After some confusion with the desk officer at South District, Gleason finally got through to Quorck.

"The desk cop insisted you didn't work there," Gleason said. "Took a couple of minutes to find you."

"I'm here on temporary duty from another district," Quorck said. "Poor guy must've missed the memo."

"Sounds like he might've worked here at one time," Gleason joked. "So what's up with this homicide you have?"

"Does the name Jules Flores mean anything to you?"

"It could," Gleason said.

"How about the Christo Mortuary? Ever hear of it?"

"Tell you what, detective," Gleason said. "It'd be much quicker if we just cut to the chase. Yeah, both names mean something to me. So once again, what's up?"

"Sorry about that," Quorck apologized. "Force of habit. The homicide I'm investigating was reported this morning. Victim's been identified as Jules Flores, though not officially. He owned the mortuary I mentioned. I called them and they said you had also phoned today asking to speak with him. I found that interesting and was wondering, as you just said, what's up?"

"Give me a second to get my head together," Gleason laughed. "This is amazing. I've got a homicide here in Key West that involves that mortuary. And, yes, I did call there earlier to speak with Flores. Person who answered the phone said he wasn't in. Now I guess I know why. Thing is, I'd talked with Flores just the other day in Miami concerning my victim. I'd invited a DEA agent in Miami to come with me then because of possible drug trafficking by someone there at the mortuary."

"Hmm," Quorck said.

"How was Flores killed?" Gleason asked.

"Single gunshot wound to the chest. Body was found early this morning on a sidewalk in an area known for...uh... occasional acts of crime and violence. Had no identification. I eventually ran him down through DMV."

"My vic took a single shot in the head," Gleason said. "Not sure that has anything to do with either homicide. Think yours was a robbery and he resisted?"

"Has the trappings but I'm not certain. The neighborhood's good for that sort of thing but there's something hinky. Can't say what's bothering me but maybe the autopsy will tell more. I'll try to put a rush on that with the coroner."

"Let's exchange cellphone numbers," Gleason suggested. "Make things easier than having to deal with your desk officer."

Gleason gave her his number and also Mike Green's. He figured they'd all be in touch with each one another sooner or later. Sam Merrill had overheard most of their conversation.

"Unbelievable," he said.

"Yeah, losing Flores is a real setback," Gleason said, getting up. "I'd better go update the lieutenant. I see he's at his desk."

Gleason took Lt. Jay Halderman through the investigation from start to the present.

"So the only person left standing that we can put our hands on is Jack Hunter," he said. "Well, you work with what you have. It always gets worse before it gets better. Especially when Hunter's involved."

"By the way," Halderman said, "the newspapers have the identification of the victim. Called me to confirm it. They also know about the drugs. Probably will name our witness next. Well, that information won't have come from the department, if they do."

"This thing's pointing more to Miami," Gleason said. "Let them deal with the news media. As far as Hunter goes, I don't think he's in any danger here."

"So how do you plan to handle the investigation, Earl?" Halderman asked. "There are two police departments and another agency involved. Stands to reason you'll need some kind of coordination."

"Haven't had to give that any thought until now, LT," Gleason said. "Every day something else seems to happen in some other damn place that's tied to this thing. Merrill has the airport and while that wasn't a homicide, the SUV was used in one. The Miami detective impresses me as being pretty sharp. Think we'll be talking some more. Mike Green has an interest in this, as well. That reminds me, I'd better call him about Flores. After all is said and done, maybe the best plan is for each of us to take care of our own end and stay in touch. Share what we can when we can. Be a virtual task force."

"I can go along with that," Halderman nodded.

"There is one other possible lead I need to follow up," Gleason said.

~~~

Jack had gone straight home from the restaurant. He thought he might drop by later this evening to catch the Troubled Birds but for the moment he was happy to just kick back on the front porch as the day wound down. His phone rang. He saw it was Gleason.

"Hello, Earl."

"Where are you?" Gleason asked.

"Sitting on my stoop watching the chickens."

"Stay there. I'm leaving the station now."

Ten minutes later a rooster and two hens scratching in the small yard scattered as Gleason drove up and parked.

"Social visit?" Jack asked.

"Business," Gleason replied gruffly.

Both men went inside the house and Gleason explained why he was there and what he wanted. It had to do with Astrid Kelly.

"She's not a suspect but certainly qualifies as a person-of-interest in this damn investigation," he said. "I need to find out where she is so I can talk with her."

"What makes you think she would tell me that?" Jack shrugged. "She's already been spooked twice by you guys."

"That's true but this time you'll be calling her," Gleason said. "And since you are an old flame, maybe you can cozy up to her."

"That flame burned out a long time ago," Jack laughed. "Not even sure if it really ever existed. Do we have to do this?"

"You going to help me or not?"

"All right, how do you want me to play it?"

"Say you've been thinking about her lately. Decided to call on the spur of the moment. Keep it light and casual. Be yourself. No, on second thought, just stick with being light and casual."

Jack scrolled down his phone to Astrid Kelly's number and dialed. It answered after four rings.

"Jack?" a familiar voice questioned. "Is this really you? I saw your number and couldn't believe it."

"Hi, Astrid," Jack said breezily. "Was just going through my phone directory and came across your number. Thought I'd see if it was still current. It's been awhile. How are you?"

"This is such a lovely surprise," she tittered. "I'm all right, Jack."

Gleason grinned. He could easily overhear.

"Long time, no see," Jack said. "In fact the last time was on my birthday at the restaurant when you dropped by with some friends. Remember? Been back to Key West since then?"

"No, and I really do miss the old place," Astrid said. "So tell me what you are up to?"

"Still hanging at the restaurant," Jack said. "Same old gang. Crazy as ever."

Gleason, who loved the theater, groaned inwardly at the hammy performance.

"Where're you living now?" Jack asked. "I'm sure it's on the boat but anywhere special? Oh, and how's Carl?"

"Actually, I'm in Bimini, Jack. Staying with good friends. You should fly over. Short hop from Miami. Be great to see you again. Make up for old times. And Carl's well, thank you. I'll tell him you asked."

"That's tempting about flying over," Jack said, cutting his eyes at Gleason. "Have you been there long, I mean you're sticking around for awhile, right? Wouldn't want to make the trip for nothing."

"Got here last month, Jack. It's a great time of the year. And my friends are wonderful people. They have room in the house or I can put you up on the boat. Wouldn't that be fun?"

"I'll give that serious thought, Astrid. You have my number?"

"I do now. Bye, Jack."

Jack exchanged a look with Gleason and ended the call.

"What do you think about that last comment about having your number?" Gleason asked. "Was she being cagey or what?"

"Could mean anything. Nothing's ever straight with Astrid. Besides, she sounded like she was high."

"So she's in Bimini," Gleason said. "Kind of complicates things."

"Ha," Jack scoffed. "So she says but I'm not sure. That was her boat I saw at Fort Zach. I checked with the harbor master afterwards. She'd left Key West on that same day. My guess is she was heading for Miami and is still there. She was lying about Bimini."

Gleason was silent for a moment.

"She could've been there on and off," Gleason said. "Sailed down here and was on her way back. Miami might be a dangerous place for her at the moment. Two people connected to this case are now dead. Well, make it three if you count the heart attack victim. The latest one was found this morning on a street in Miami. He'd been shot."

Jack was shocked at hearing of a third death.

"Who was it?" he asked.

"Guy who owned the hearse," Gleason told him. "But why don't you believe Astrid's in Bimini. Maybe she really does have friends there."

"If she does have friends in Bimini, she's not there with them at the moment," Jack said. "Maybe she has plans for going later. But that was all an act. She doesn't know Carl Napier is dead. My bet is she's still waiting for him to show up in Miami. And you're right. She could be in more danger than she realizes."

"I suppose that could be true about her not knowing Napier's dead," Gleason said. "Although maybe not for long. The paper has his name. They'll probably run a big story on him. Could be she'll see it. Like you said, they could've planned on going to Bimini after the drug deal. For now it was a good cover. Top of the mind."

"Anything and everything is top-of-mind with Astrid," Jack said. "Was this stupid charade helpful?"

"We learned one thing," Gleason said. "She'll take a phone call from you."

Chapter 16

Detective Keisha Quorck had returned to the apartment building and had sought out the superintendent. She'd brought Jules Flores' photo with her and the man had been hesitant to identify it as the person living there. She had then explained that a homicide was involved and it would be to everyone's benefit for him to cooperate.

"Just trying to respect people's privacy is all," he said glumly. "Hardly any left these days. Management has a pretty strict rule about that."

"I appreciate your feelings, sir," Quorck sympathized. "And I understand your position. Can you tell me if Mr. Flores lived here alone?"

Another delay.

"Sir?"

"He wasn't married, if that's what you mean. No missus listed on his mailbox anyway. Otherwise I wouldn't know anything about his personal life."

"Thank you. I would like to see the apartment," Quorck said.

"I'd have to get permission and the office is closed," the man told her. "Probably want a warrant or something, too."

"Hmm…" Quorck said. "Then I'd better get a warrant. Probably be after midnight before it's approved. I'll station some uniformed officers in the lobby and on Mr. Flores' floor for security while we're waiting. We'll try not to disturb the residents too much. Like you said, there's not much privacy anymore. Don't want to use up what little we have."

The man shifted uneasily on his feet.

"How long will you take to see the apartment?" he asked.

"Be long gone before anyone knows I've even been here," Quorck whispered with a wink.

They took the elevator to the eleventh floor, which offered splendid views of Biscayne Bay and beyond from huge windows at either end of the hallway.

"All the apartments have electronic door locks now," the man said, as they walked down the hall. "Much better security than a key. We re-issue the cards every month. Including the ones for the staff."

They came to the last apartment and he swiped a keycard across the lock.

"From what I understand, this unit was built specially for one of the original investors," the man said. "Only one bedroom but it's really nice. Supposed to have been some drug money involved when they built it. Lot of that around back then. Had to put it somewhere, I suppose. They were throwing these things up like crazy."

He opened the door. The whole apartment had been tossed.

"Don't go in there, sir," Quorck said quickly, placing a hand on his arm.

"What the hell's going on here?" he said, shocked by the mess. "The office isn't going to like this. I'd better call their emergency number. Get somebody over here."

"You do that, sir," she said, "but this apartment is now a possible crime scene. It's off limits to everyone for the time being. I need you to go back downstairs to the lobby and make your call from there. Some police officers will soon be arriving. Please direct them up here, okay?"

The man hurriedly left and Quorck phoned her boss in detectives at South District. She explained the situation, saying she was certain no one was in the apartment but she wouldn't enter until patrol arrived as backup. She also requested a crime scene specialist to dust for fingerprints and to take photos. That done, she waited outside the door and took in the apartment.

The foyer opened into a large living area overlooking Biscayne Bay. A serving bar separated the room from a small kitchen. She noted a hallway which she assumed led to the bedroom.

She heard the elevator door slide open and turned to see two uniformed officers step out.

"This way, gentlemen," she called.

~~~

The Troubled Birds were setting up their equipment at the Undrinkable Bar while Jack watched from the side. They'd all arrived at about the same time and he had offered to help but had been politely refused. After a final sound check and everything had met with their satisfaction, they joined him at the bar.

"Get you anything?" he asked.

"Just water for me, luv," Tina said with an accent that Jack had to bend an ear to fully understand.

She was the bassist in the group. Krysta played guitar and Angela was on drums.

"Same here, luv," the other two chimed in unison.

"Save the hard stuff for after the show," Krysta joked.

Jack could certainly attest to that, remembering the night they'd casually dropped by from the Schooner.

"Billy told us about the awful thing that happened to you," Krysta said. "Can't imagine something like that. Have they arrested the bloody wanker?"

God, Jack thought, is there anyone Billy hasn't told?

"Don't know," he said. "He wasn't from here. Cops think he could be from Miami."

"Blimey," Angela giggled. "He could've been in one of the clubs we played."

Jack pulled out his cellphone and scrolled to the photo of the suspect's sketch. He'd never understood why he would even have wanted the thing in the first place. Just somehow it had mattered to him at the time.

"Here, take a look," he said, showing her the photo. "Recognize him?"

"What is that?" Angela asked.

"It's a drawing the police sketch artist made of the suspect from my description," Jack explained.

The three women stared at the picture.

"Mean little eyes," Tina said. "Makes me shudder."

"Made me, too," Jack agreed.

Krista frowned.

"He kinda reminds me of that snide beaut at Footprints," she said. "Remember him?"

"Now that you mention it, yeah," Tina said.

"What's a beaut and where is Footprints?" Jack asked.

Krysta laughed.

"Sorry, luv," she said. "A beaut's what we call an idiot. Footprints is a bar in Miami. On the river which is about the only thing it has going for it. Just another dive bar of the bloody ilk we've played lately. Anyway, this beaut saunters over from the bar. I figured him for making a request, see? Instead, he grabs his crotch and blows me a kiss. I flipped him the finger and told him to go jerk off in the little boys' room. There's always one in every audience, you know? His mates at the bar were bevied up—that means drunk—and they laughed their arses off. Didn't take to that too much, he didn't."

"When was that?" Jack asked.

"Couple of weeks before we came down here," Krista said.

"Would you mind telling the police what you just told me?" Jack asked. "I think it might be a help."

"Wouldn't mind at all, luv. We'll take all the publicity we can get."

~~~

Quorck suspected the only fingerprints that might be relative would be on the apartment's entrance. Still she had the technician dust every surface inside that looked promising but to pay particular attention to both sides of the door, including the jambs and the knobs.

They'd been there for nearly four hours and had found nothing that would explain why the place had been so trashed. She had ruled out burglary. There were too many valuables not to have been taken. Nice set of silverware and a fancy silver candelabrum. Gold cufflinks and a few other trinkets in a pulled-out drawer. Even some cash in another one. No self-respecting thief would've passed that up.

The thought had occurred to her that maybe Flores was just a messy person but she soon dismissed it. It was obvious that someone had come here looking for something. Even the sloppiest of slobs wouldn't live like this. The question is, what were they were looking for and did they find it?

"You have enough pictures?" she asked the crime scene photographer.

"I'm good to go," the officer said.

"Okay, let's call it a night," she said. "Thanks everyone. I'm going to hang here a little while longer."

The tiny group gathered themselves up and left. Quorck shut the door behind them. Alone now, she walked over to the huge living room window and looked out on the bay. Key Biscayne sparkled distantly like a jewel set in the black water.

What would it be like to live in a place like this, she wondered. How long before you took the view for granted? She thought of her tiny one side of a duplex in Opa-Locka with a view of the street. Well, it suited her fine and the neighbors were nice.

More to the point, what the hell was going on with this thing she had on her hands now? Nothing seemed to add up. She began ticking off the facts they knew so far.

One, an unidentified body found shot dead on a sidewalk. Signs pointing to either a drug deal or a robbery gone bad. Her personal jury was still out on that one.

Two, victim ID'd as Jules Flores, owner of a mortuary.

Three, Flores turns out to be a person-of-interest in a Key West homicide investigation where drugs were indeed involved.

And now, someone has broken into his damn apartment. Well, not exactly broken in. The door didn't appear to have been forced open. You needed an electronic keycard to enter.

So who would have one of those besides Flores? The building superintendent, cleaning people, management…his assailant?

Flores' wallet was missing. Maybe his keycard was in it. The drivers license would've shown his posh address. Person could've come looking for more.

But nothing of value was taken. Quorck felt she was going in circles.

She realized she hadn't noticed any security cameras in the hallway and made a mental note to ask the superintendent. Should've thought about that earlier. What was wrong with her?

Her head was beginning to hurt. She looked at her watch. It wasn't all that late. She took out her phone and punched in Gleason's number.

Chapter 17

Sam Merrill was at his desk in the detectives room when Gleason arrived.

"Crime lab did themselves proud, Earl," he said. "Wait 'til you see."

"Running a little behind this morning," Gleason grumbled. "Up half the night on the phone. What do you have?"

"Shooter's new composite came in. Check your computer."

Gleason sat down and scrolled to the site.

"Outstanding," he said. "At least, it looks more realistic."

"Be interesting to hear what your star witness thinks of it," Merrill said.

Gleason picked up his cellphone.

"Let's find out," he said. "I'll tell him to expect an email."

His phone rang before he could scroll to the number. He recognized the caller ID.

"Speak of the devil," he answered. "I was about to call you, Hunter. Got an enhanced picture of the shooter I want you look at."

"Must be great minds at work," Jack said. "I was calling to tell you I might have another line on him."

He then explained in detail his conversation with the Troubled Birds at the Undrinkable Bar.

Gleason was flabbergasted. He didn't know which part of the story was more implausible, but considering who was doing the telling, anything was possible.

"Nobody was drinking or anything like that?" he asked suspiciously.

"This was before their first set," Jack said. "They never have a drink until after they've finished for the night. And they don't do drugs."

"And they'll talk with us, you're sure?" Gleason confirmed, looking over to Merrill and giving him a thumbs up. "When can they come in?"

"I'll give them a call right now. They're staying at a motel not too far from here. I'll drive them to the station."

Gleason hung up and rubbed his forehead.

"Good news?" Merrill asked.

"Some troubled birds think they've seen our shooter," Gleason said. "Hunter's bringing them here."

~~~

The Straits Motel was on a short street in the quieter side of Key West. It was a throwback to old Key West. Nothing worked well half the time and the other half it was completely broken. The amenities were few but it was clean and the rates were somewhat reasonable. Jack had once taken temporary refuge there when it'd become too dangerous for him to be in his own house due to his raising embarrassing questions about an old crime that someone had preferred remain unanswered.

He'd mentioned that he'd spent a few nights at the Straits to the Troubled Birds—leaving out the reason for it—when he'd learned they had coincidentally taken up residence there since coming to town.

The women had been sunning at the tiny swimming pool when Jack had called. They'd quickly dressed for the occasion and were waiting out front as he pulled up.

"Brings back memories," he said, wistfully taking in the motel.

"Hope they're good ones, luv," Tina laughed. "Can't say I'll have many. My room's no bigger than a broom closet. Walls made of paper. You can hear the crapper flush in the loo next door."

"Yeah, it is a cheesy little place," Angela put in. "Though the pool's a treat."

"Well, at least the price is right," Krysta said. "Better than those bloody scalpers in Miami. What's this Gleason bloke like we're going to see?"

"He has an amusing sense of humor," Jack smiled.

They all piled into the Jeep, Krista offering once more to drive them there in their own car, Jack refusing once again.

"Hey, this is fun," Angela yelled excitedly from the back seat as they roared away.

~~~

Detective Keisha Quorck yawned and sipped her coffee. Despite the late night, she'd gotten to her desk early this morning. Her conversation with the Key West detective had covered a lot of ground but instead of getting any answers, she'd merely come away with more questions.

And the coroner's report on Jules Flores that she was currently pouring over was continuing to raise them. It'd been waiting in her computer when she'd arrived at the station.

She'd learned officially that the victim had died from a gunshot wound in the chest. That a single bullet had pierced the heart and lodged in the spine. Powder burns on the skin around the entrance wound indicated it'd been fired at close range. Lividity suggested that the body had been moved. That had been the most curious part.

Blood can begin to settle in the lowest point as soon as twenty minutes after death. There it pools and eventually presents a red discoloration of the skin. Usually that takes a couple of hours before it can be seen with the naked eye and is most prominent twelve hours later. The discoloration was clearly visible on Jules Flores' backside, yet his body was found lying face down.

Yes, obviously the murder was done elsewhere. She'd had a feeling about that at the scene. Explained the missing casing, too. Six-shooters notwithstanding.

She took another sip of coffee.

But why was the body loaded into a car afterwards—more likely some time afterwards considering the state of lividity—driven to Liberty City and dumped out in the street? Stripped of identification and a possible wristwatch? Was this done purposely? To make it look like a robbery? Yes, possibly. But again, why?

There had to be some significance in such a brazen and callous act but for the life of her she couldn't see it.

The coffee was giving her a sour taste. She fished out a pack of chewing gum from her purse and unwrapped a stick. What she'd really like was a cigarette but it had been three months now since she'd quit and she'd be damned if she was going to give in to the urge.

The slug that'd killed Flores had remained fairly intact, the report said, and was being sent to the crime lab for ballistics. She would follow up on that.

Since drugs were involved in the Key West homicide and her victim was regarded as a person-of-interest in that investigation, she might get some more questions to puzzle over from the Miami DEA. She picked up her cellphone and called Agent Mike Green.

Chapter 18

Astrid Kelly dusted her pinky finger with finely chopped cocaine and massaged her gums with it. The trick produced a nice enough high and Lord knows, her nose could use a timeout from snorting the stuff. Lately, her sinuses had been on a rampage. On the practical side, she'd found that gumming was less wasteful than sniffing it up your nose, especially if you happened to sneeze at the moment. That'd also been happening with regularity lately. And her supply was getting a little low.

Feeling somewhat relaxed she poured a glass of wine and took it up to the deck. Normally, she wasn't a morning drinker but as her long-departed fiancé used to joke, it was happy hour somewhere.

The *Justice* was berthed between two larger sailboats at the Miami marina. One belonged to a live-aboard family with two bratty kids who couldn't get along together, the other appeared empty. She hadn't seen anyone around it anyway. This particular marina was a new experience for her. She'd always docked farther south when she had reason to be in Miami. Carl had made the arrangements this time.

Her dock-neighbor's rotten children were involved in a noisy game of some sort, so she made her way forward to the bow where it was quieter and settled down on a cushion. Key Biscayne lay across the bay. She shaded her eyes with her hand to see if she could spot Edwardo Grubber's apartment building. She remembered that it was in a cluster toward the end. She hadn't been there since the time they'd all sailed to Key West. What a horrible trip that had turned out to be. And it had started out so marvelously.

Edwardo and Lisa had recently bought the apartment then and were back in town to celebrate. Edwardo had business in Honduras and traveled often to Miami. She'd first met the couple during a short stay herself in Havana and had become friends with Lisa.

After the Key West fiasco she'd thought she would never hear from them again. Naturally, she had been surprised when a friend of his had phoned to ask if she would do a favor for Edwardo. It wouldn't go unappreciated, he'd assured. She'd been a little leery after hearing what was involved until Carl pointed out that the chance to make a quick and easy twenty-thousand dollars didn't come along all that often. And reminded her that the boat's last haul-out had cost her a ton. Told her not to worry, that he'd handle everything. Just sit back and leave it to him.

Well, he was certainly right about the money she had spent on the boat. However, that'd been necessary. Boats are money pits. So she'd taken him for his word and left the details to him. And now where was dear old Carl? Still in Key West, if one can believe those two ridiculous telephone calls from him. Well, she was beginning to have serious doubts.

She looked at the empty wine glass. She should've brought the bottle with her. Nothing else to do but go below and get it.

The stupid bottle was nearly empty. She poured what remained into her glass and decided not to go back up. The sun had begun to bear down and it was much more comfortable here.

An unsettling thought crossed her mind. Was she being played for a fool? They were supposed to get the money in Key West. But that awful man said that everything would be settled in Miami. Carl had been all too happy to drive that creepy hearse when that other man got sick. Said that would help him keep an eye on things. Had he now done a runner on her?

She'd left her stash on the galley table. She drew a forefinger through the remaining white powder and stuck it in her mouth.

Another thought occurred. If there'd been an accident involving a hearse, surely that would've made the news. She grabbed up her phone. Her real phone, not that cheap thing they'd been using during this silly business. This was a newer model Carl had gotten from who knows where. She was able to keep her old number, too. At least she could trust any calls she got now. She wasn't familiar with all of its features but knew enough to get on the web. She went to the Key West Citizen's site. A few more scrolls and there was her answer.

~~~

The front desk officer had called Gleason to tell him that his guests had arrived. Merrill said he'd go get them, that it'd be good to stretch his legs. He soon returned with a suppressed grin on his face, three women and Jack Hunter.

"Hello, Earl," Jack greeted. "Like you to meet the Troubled Birds. This is Krysta, Tina, Angela."

They were wearing identical black short-shorts and yellow halter-tops with square necklines showing just enough skin to be naughty but nice. Stylish sandals with a slight rise at the heels added a little more definition to their legs.

"And ladies, this is Detective Earl Gleason," Jack said with a flourish.

All three women curtsied.

Gleason stood up from his desk, feeling slightly bewildered, not to mention embarrassed.

"Thank you all for coming here," he said. "I understand you may have some information."

"Jack showed us a picture of the bloke you're looking for," Tina told him excitedly. "We might've seen him. Acting like a bloody beaut, he was."

"Ta," Krysta agreed. "Real gobshite."

"You ladies are from Liverpool," Merrill said in surprise. "My granddad on my mom's side was a scouser."

They flashed him a big smile.

Gleason gave him a puzzled look.

"Scouser's what they call people from there," Merrill explained to Gleason. "He lived with us when I was a kid so I grew up hearing it. Another language, man. Gobshite is an annoying person, by the way."

Gleason cleared his throat.

"Well, we have a new and improved picture of that person you may have seen," he said, bringing up the photo on his computer. "Take a look."

Jack and all three women stared at the screen.

"Isn't that him, Krysta?" Tina asked.

"That's the bloke," Krysta agreed, nodding.

"What do you think, Hunter?" Gleason asked.

Jack stood silently taking in the image, his thoughts having returned to the crime scene and the pitiless murder he'd witnessed, stark and indelibly imprinted in his mind.

"That's the bloke," he said tightly.

"Good," Gleason grinned. "I'll get this new print off to the Miami department. They can also check out that bar. What's its name again, ladies?"

"Footprints," Krysta told him.

"Got an address?" Gleason asked.

"It's in downtown Miami off 7th Avenue," Jack answered. "By the river. I looked it up. Footprints is also the title of a great little piece Miles Davis worked on. Just a bit of music trivia."

A familiar foreboding crept into Gleason's gut.

~~~

DEA Agent Mike Green had expressed an interest in seeing Jules Flores' apartment during the phone call with Detective Keisha Quorck. They'd decided to meet at the building and were now in the superintendent's office.

"I meant to ask you this when I was last here, sir," Quorck said to the man. "Are there security cameras in the building? I didn't notice any."

"Board voted to have them removed," he told her. "Violation of privacy. Sensitive subject these days."

"Ah, yes, that old privacy problem again," Quorck smiled. "Before we go up, could you tell me if Mr. Flores had a parking space? I'd like to see it, providing that isn't violating any issues."

"Name's on the wall behind the space," he said wearily. "You can take the elevator down to the garage."

"Thank you," Quorck said. "We won't be long. Then you can take us upstairs and let us in the apartment."

The superintendent momentarily closed his eyes and nodded.

"What do you hope to find?" Green asked as they got on the elevator.

"Hmm…good question. Don't really know. Sometimes I just leave everything to my better angels and hope for the best."

The elevator stopped and they stepped out into the parking area. Only three automobiles were there.

"Not very busy today," Quorck observed.

"Yeah, but check out that baby," Green said, pointing at a red Ferrari. "Must've cost a couple hundred grand."

"High-priced neighborhood," Quorck shrugged. "Flores owned a Mercedes. There's his space up ahead. Next to the last one on this side."

"Lot of room between the spaces." Green commented. "Make sure no one doors your pricey toy, I guess."

"I don't see anything," Quorck said disappointedly, standing in front of the empty parking space. "Shucks, I was expecting to find a locker full of answers. So much for my angels. Let's go up to the apartment."

"Wait a minute, Keisha," Green said, pointing at a dark stain on the floor in the adjacent space. "What's that over there?"

"Could it be from a car?" Quorck asked. "My car's always dripping something messy."

"Doesn't appear to be oil or grease," he said. "I could be wrong but I think it's dried blood,"

A chill rippled down Quorck's back.

"If so, I've a feeling this may be where Jules Flores was last alive," she said tensely. "I'll get some crime scene people here."

Thirty minutes had passed before anyone showed up. She'd requested a forensic team, a photographer and a couple of uniformed patrol officers. Green had gone back upstairs to wait for them. Quorck had remained in the parking garage.

While there she'd paced off the entire area. And jotted down the license plates of the three cars parked there. Including the names of the owners. She'd run them through the state motor vehicle department rather than fight with the building management for any more information. She doubted if she'd learn much from them, although she'd been lucky with longer shots in the past.

But a remarkable piece of good luck had indeed come her way. She'd discovered a brass casing lying on the floor not far from the neighboring parking space. She'd placed a glassine envelope over it for protection. It'd be officially marked and photographed when the team arrived.

A two-man patrol car was the first on the scene and she stationed one officer at the garage entrance to secure it and the other in the lobby to explain what was going on if anyone asked. She also had the elevator temporarily taken out of service to prevent any unwanted intrusions, much to the superintendent's protestations.

Ten minutes later the forensics team rolled up out front. Green directed them around the side driveway to the garage.

Quorck wasn't sure a fingerprint taker was necessary but she was covering all bases. Especially since there'd been no security cameras, which still stung her. Definitely the crime scene photographer would be of good use. She filled them in and they went to work.

"Dried blood's a bugger to type, detective," the technician complained after examining the stain. "Doesn't dry in a uniform way. Gets unstable. All sorts of bad things happen to blood once it's out in the open. Not saying it can't be done, just it ain't easy."

"Can you get DNA from this stain?" Quorck asked.

"That's tricky, too," he answered. "Really labor intensive process. Lot of protocols to follow. Like I said, they don't make it easy in this business."

This guy practically exudes pessimism, Quorck thought to herself. She'd never run into anyone quite like him. She searched her mind for a last straw of hope before she threw up her hands in frustration. She couldn't find one.

"So what can be done?" she asked, almost tearfully.

"Well, there is this little test and it's fairly accurate, too," he said. "Tells you if we're looking at human or animal blood."

"I'll buy it," she said brightly. "And I expect you and the entire crime lab to use whatever scientific voodoo it takes to get me that DNA, too."

Another hour passed and the team finished up. Quorck released everyone, the parking garage was opened and the elevator put back in service, all much to the relief of the superintendent. She and Green rode with him up to Flores' floor.

"How much longer does this thing have to stay here?" he asked, referring to the yellow police tape plastered on the apartment door. "Been getting some complaints."

"We want it taken down as much as you do, sir," Quorck said. "We appreciate your patience in the meantime."

He swiped the card key at the lock and pushed the door open.

"It's all yours," he said tiredly. "I'll be downstairs if you need me."

Nothing had been touched since Quorck was last there.

"Sorry about the mess," she said, stepping inside. "I didn't expect company."

"You should see my place," Green rejoined.

"Anywhere special you want to start?" Quorck asked.

"I'd like to just walk around first," Green said, slipping on a pair of gloves. "I know they've dusted for prints but I like to be careful."

Quorck took in the view of Key Biscayne while Green busied himself.

"Nice little stash of money in this drawer," he called out from the bedroom. "Must be several hundred bucks at least."

"Yeah, your generic burglar wouldn't have passed up that," Quorck said.

"Well, somebody was definitely looking for something of value to him," Green said, returning to the living room.

"This whole thing's getting nuttier by the minute," Quorck said. "If that blood stain in the garage belongs to Flores, he was obviously shot there and then his apartment gone through. I don't think he would've stood around watching someone tear up the place and then have gone back down with him to be killed. And how did he get here? His car's parked at the mortuary."

"He could have been picked up there or even somewhere else and driven here," Green said. "Could've been more than one person involved, too."

"Hmm…that's interesting," Quorck said. "Let's say two people grabbed Flores at the mortuary or wherever. Drove him here. One waits with him in the garage while the other goes up to ransack the apartment. But then why shoot him after he'd finished and dump the body in Liberty City?"

"Maybe they found what they wanted and they no longer needed him," Green said.

"It must have been in the last place they looked then," Quorck said, gesturing to the trashed room. "Still doesn't explain Liberty City."

"Sending a message?" Green suggested.

"Well…okay, but what were they trying to say and who were they saying it to?"

"This is a stretch," Green said. "I've been thinking about Gleason's homicide victim. He knew Edwardo Grubber, who's a kingpin in the Honduran cartel. I don't know how well he knew him or whether they were friends but let that ride for now. He was driving the hearse with the drugs. We assumed they were for Grubber. But suppose they weren't. Flores seemed surprised when he was told there'd been a different driver than the one he'd sent. More so, he was rattled. Suppose Flores was trafficking on the sly.

Grubber gets wind of it and not only has him murdered but dumps him on the street like he was garbage. No respect."

"Flores's wallet was missing," Quorck said. "Might've been wearing a watch, too. First impression was it'd been a robbery."

"I don't think so," Green said. "I believe they were making a point. Word gets around in that circle. Maybe a late-night passerby took the watch and wallet. When Gleason and I talked with Flores, he was wearing an expensive looking watch. Would've been tempting to take off someone lying in the street, if you didn't give a damn."

"I'll ask robbery to keep an eye out," Quorck said. "Check the pawnshops, too."

"I realize this is all speculation but some of it might be on target," Green said. "The other thing with Gleason's homicide was that his witness said the suspect appeared ready to shoot him but instead just spit at him and left. No respect shown there, either. He wasn't even worth shooting. How about that?"

"That witness should've gone out immediately afterwards and bought a lottery ticket." Quorck said.

"He's a pretty cool guy," Green said. "I met him once. I've finished with everything I need here. You okay to go?"

"Sure, I might head back to the station."

"Yeah, I have to hit my office, too," Green said. "Try not to be there long. Taking my wife to dinner tonight at that new restaurant in the Grove. It's our wedding anniversary."

"Then you should go straight home from here," Quorck admonished.

"Sound advice, Detective. Think I'll take you up on it."

Chapter 19

Jack had dropped off the Troubled Birds at the Straits Motel, saying he'd see them tonight at the Undrinkable Bar. They'd made a big fuss again urging him to bring his saxophone and sit in on a few numbers. He'd promised he would think about it.

But instead of driving home, he had headed for Stock Island, stopping at Fausto's on the way to pick up some deli and a couple of beers. He'd suddenly felt a need to spend a little time with himself.

Now he was sitting on the deck of the *Joyful Noise* watching the sky redden in the west. He could almost hear Bobby Sunshine comment on it, stepping out of the wheelhouse to join him.

"Red sky at night, sailor's delight. Red sky at morning, sailor take warning," the old man would've said.

He smiled at the adage. Bobby Sunshine was full of them and would take one out to use at every opportunity. He missed his cantankerous friend. He missed Ruth LaVere's sanctimony. Then there was little Roy. How long did parrots live?

His life had certainly taken a different path since the last time he'd been on this boat.

A couple passing by waved to him.

"Nice sunset," one of them called out.

"Delightful," Jack replied.

Rachel Powers' letter came to mind. Actually, it had never left. Just kicked around in his head stirring up old memories and suggesting new and disturbing possibilities.

Recently, he had begun to paint a rosier picture of their future. She wasn't saying goodbye after all, only letting him know that things might be quiet on her end for awhile. Not by choice but by necessity.

It was the return address that'd led him to that line of thinking. The infantry regiment she was serving with didn't seem to exist.

He hadn't recognized the outfit as any he'd been familiar with when he'd been in the Army. Maybe it was part of a new reorganization. The Army had changed since then. He didn't even want to think how many years had passed since he'd been a grunt. He'd been curious, nonetheless, and had looked the unit up. Wasn't listed as belonging to any division or as a separate unit that he could find. And he'd checked with a number of sources.

His thinking had then taken a short step over to conspiracy theory. It had to be a spook address, he'd reasoned. Clandestine units probably used them. Which meant she could be anywhere. And not necessarily overseas but just as easily at a military base here. Perhaps working undercover to root out insurrectionists in the service.

The stronger possibility, and the one most likely to be true, finally showed up and took charge. Coping with the pandemic had left a lot of people wacky. Isolation and separation can do that to you. A few of *his* marbles may have slipped out of the bag over time and had temporarily rearranged his brain. His synapse wasn't snapping.

The painful reality he'd at last come to accept was that the letter meant exactly what it said. Nothing more and nothing less. No farfetched reasoning would change that painful fact And life would go on regardless. For both of them.

And to be truthful, he wanted life to go on. His own had been on the edge of ending not all that long ago. Call it luck or what, he'd come within a whisker of joining Carl Napier on the last flight out.

The sunset having completed its act, night now had taken the stage and had begun to sprinkle a few stars across the sky.

Jack had drunk only half a bottle of beer and had barely touched his dinner. He poured the beer over the side and tucked the full bottle in a bag with the rest of the food. He'd take it home for later.

He secured the *Joyful Noise* and left for the Undrinkable Bar.

~~~

Detective Keisha Quorck hadn't stayed at the station very long after returning. Nothing new to keep her there. Too early for any ballistics results from the crime lab. She'd written her report on the day's activities and submitted it to her boss. No word from down south. She didn't know what she expected to hear from the Key West detective anyway. Funny, she'd felt kind of sad that he hadn't called.

She had chosen a classic Western for tonight's movie and a rather long one at that. *The Treasure of the Sierra Madre.*

She munched on a raw carrot in the kitchen while the popcorn popper rat-a-tat-tatted an uneven rhythm. She'd put in half a cup of corn, which would be more than enough to fill her largest bowl. She'd go easy on the salt and absolutely no butter.

A last final and slower rat-a-tat-tat and the popcorn was ready. She poured it out, filling the bowl to overflowing. Not a single kernel was burnt. She would clean up after the movie.

She settled on the sofa and was reaching for the remote to turn on the television set when her phone rang. A moment of decision. Let it go to message or answer? The caller ID demanded she answer.

"Good evening, Detective Gleason," she said. "To borrow a phrase from you, what's up?"

"Got some news from the crime lab I thought you'd be interested in hearing," Gleason said. "The same gun killed both of our victims. Ballistics matched the two slugs."

Quorck straightened up from her slouch.

"I was in the station earlier," she said. "Nothing from them came for me."

"Maybe they finished mine first," Gleason said. "I don't know. But now we're both looking for the same suspect. What's the chance of us getting together and comparing notes?"

"Your place or mine?"

"Let me come up there," Gleason opted. "Time we met each other face to face anyway. Mike Green should be in on this, too."

"I agree," Quorck said. "Coincidently, Agent Mike Green and I were at Jules Flores' apartment today for a look around. I now think Flores might've been murdered in the building's parking garage. There was a bloodstain on the floor. I had forensic come to take a look. Also, I found a casing there. Sent it to the crime lab."

"They also have the casing from my scene," Gleason said. "Matchup there will put another lock on proving it was the same gun."

"Would tomorrow morning around nine be convenient?" Quorck asked.

"Christ, I'd have to leave here before five to get there," Gleason said. "How about ten?"

"That can work. I'm in South District. The station's located in Coconut Grove."

"I know where it is," Gleason said. "I'll call Green."

"He's having dinner out with his wife tonight," Quorck said. "It's their anniversary. I'll call him first thing in the morning."

Gleason laughed.

"I certainly wouldn't want to disturb the celebration," he said. "See you tomorrow. Hope your coffee's better than ours."

"Bring some doughnuts," Quorck said. "I like chocolate."

Gleason hung up. Quorck took a handful of popcorn from the bowl. It was still warm but she felt too excited to watch any movie tonight.

~~~

Jack had stopped by his house to pick up his saxophone before continuing to the restaurant. The unopened beer went into the refrigerator, his half-eaten dinner went into the garbage can along with the empty bottle he'd brought back.

The Troubled Birds had already set up by the time he arrived. They weren't due to play for another fifteen minutes and were sitting at the bar dressed to kill in their black shorts and yellow halter tops.

"Top of the evening, luv," Tina said. "Don't tell me there's a musical instrument in that little box under your arm."

"Yeah," Jack grinned, as he opened the case. "It's an old Selmer soprano I found at a garage sale years ago and had rebuilt. Real antique but it still has a sweet sound."

"Isn't that just the most darling thing," Krysta cooed. "Come on, luv. I'll give you a tuning note on me axe."

Jack followed her to the bandstand.

A couple of plucks and toots put the little horn in fine fettle. Jack rifted through a blues scale.

"Oh, I like that," Krysta purred. "Maybe we can get down with some blues tonight instead of just rock."

Jack smiled. Life goes on.

~~~

Astrid Kelly fumbled around in the dark cabin. This was so confusing. She'd closed her eyes for only a second. She could've sworn it had been no more than a minute ago and it had been bright daylight then. When did it get to be night?

She stumbled over something. Catching herself on the galley table and getting her bearings, she reached for the light switch and flicked it on.

Stuff was strewn about. An empty wine bottle lay on the floor. That was probably what had tripped her. She sat down at the table and tried to remember.

She recalled reading the newspaper article on her phone about the accident. Naturally, that had upset her. And now to think their perfect plan all had been for nothing. What a screwup!

She should never have had anything to do with this ridiculous thing. Why did she ever listen to Carl? And look where it had gotten him? They should've stayed where they were at that nice marina in Naples instead of sailing off to Mexico.

Suddenly, a cringe-worthy memory surfaced with crystal clarity.

She had phoned Edwardo Grubber on the private number his wife had given her. Blabbed everything about what had gone on and demanded that he pay the twenty thousand dollars she was owed. It wasn't her fault that he didn't get his stupid drugs. He'd asked where she was and she had foolishly told him.

Now her feral instincts were telling her that'd she might have made a big mistake.

Fright swept over her.

What if he sent that man from Key West? He had to be the person who'd killed Carl. He certainly wouldn't be coming with any money for her. She had to leave but she wasn't in any kind of shape to sail. Still, she couldn't stay here.

Fingertips pressed hard against her temples, she desperately hoped an idea might pop out.

And just like that, one did.

She lowered her hands and calmly went to gather some blankets. She next turned off the lights, locked the cabin and hid the key. And with blankets in hand, she walked next door to the boat with no one aboard.

Chapter 20

Gleason had been up and dressed since five a.m. He'd put down a bowl of cat food and some extra water. He had left the deck door slightly ajar in case Mitts wanted to go out and stare at the birds. The cat could also get back in to use the litter box.

In truth, he wouldn't mind if the litter box just stayed on the deck. Be less messy, probably a lot more sanitary, too. Definitely less smelly. But then he'd have to keep the door open all the time. One of those enclosed litter boxes he had seen advertised on television might even be a better idea. Cat steps inside and does its business. When he's finished, the box automatically freshens things up. Modern times. He'd look into that when he returned from Miami.

He checked his watch once more and decided to just go ahead and leave. It's a little over a four-hour drive to Miami even at the best of times. The weather report had forecasted possible rain in the area. Definitely would slow things down.

He headed out.

Not much traffic on the road this early he'd noticed passing through Sugarloaf Key. Not much open, either. Christ, was he going to have wait until Marathon for a cup of coffee? He should've filled a thermos. There were the damn doughnuts he'd promised to bring, too. Chocolate, if he remembered correctly.

He picked up his speed.

~~~

A hundred miles ahead, a small vanguard of rain had arrived in the Miami area. The heavy stuff would soon follow.

But for the moment, a pitter-patter of droplets had been enough to awaken Astrid Kelly, who'd been sound asleep on the deck of the neighboring sailboat. She pulled the blanket tighter around herself and curled into a ball.

It was no use. The rain had gotten harder and was puddling. Soon it would soak through her blanket. Why hadn't the idiotic owner put down carpeting on the deck? Wouldn't be any puddles then and it would certainly be a lot more comfortable to lie on. Never mind that her boat's deck was also bare teakwood.

She couldn't return to the *Justice*. The man might show up at any time. Could even be waiting there now. She shivered at the thought. The cold rain added some extra shivers on its own. All she had on was a bathing suit. She spotted what appeared to be a folded tarpaulin stowed by the cabin door. Also, the roof there had a slight overhang which might offer more protection than where she was presently bunked. She moved over to the cabin and wrapped herself in the canvas. Now snug in her new cocoon, she drifted back to sleep.

~~~

Traffic had come to a standstill in Key Largo. Gleason figured there had to have been an accident somewhere up the road. No telling how long the highway would be blocked. He was almost to the Route 905 turnoff which skirted around US 1. He pulled into the outside emergency lane and drove to the intersection. It'd be longer in miles this way but the Card Sound causeway might be faster.

And he had been almost right. There was hardly any holdup until he'd come to Mosquito Creek where the road had flooded all the way across. Fortunately, the water wasn't deep and the cars could slowly make it through. He picked up US 1 again at Florida City.

He wondered if Quorck had gotten in touch with Mike Green. He took out his cell and placed a call himself.

"Good morning, Earl," Green answered.

"Hi, Mike. Just checking if you got the word on our meeting. Was going to call you last night but the Miami detective said it was your anniversary and you were out to dinner. Said she'd would call you this morning."

"Yeah, spoke with her earlier. You're bringing the doughnuts, right?"

"That's questionable," Gleason laughed. "Haven't found a store yet."

"Where are you?"

"Kendall."

"Great little bakery in Coconut Grove. Red's Doughnuts. On the main drag near where we had lunch. Can't miss it. Get me a couple of jelly rolls, will you?"

~~~

Key West was all sunshine and blue skies.

Jack stood at Harbor Place in Truman Annex, appreciating a view of strikingly blue water undisturbed to the knife-edge horizon. He'd read somewhere that thousands of years ago Florida's western shore had reached a hundred miles farther out into the Gulf of Mexico from where it was now. Hard to imagine that today standing on this two-by-four mile chunk of an island.

Harbor Place had always held an attraction for him. He'd almost been ready to buy a condo in the building at one time. It wasn't that he had regretted not following through. He was satisfied with where he presently lived. Didn't change the fact that this was a lovely location, though.

He turned and continued his walk. He had no particular destination in mind. He'd awakened early and with nothing planned, had taken advantage of the beautiful morning.

His session with the Troubled Birds last night had been a lot of fun. The soprano sax was a good fit. But the blues notwithstanding, the group's forte was solid rock and after a couple of numbers he'd decided to leave them to what they did best and took a seat at the bar to enjoy the show. It'd been a good decision and they'd brought down the house for the rest of the evening.

During a break he'd asked them about Footprints. Said the name sounded like it might've been a jazz club. What was the crowd like?

They'd laughed. Said the crowd there was no different from that in any other bar. A mix of regulars, a few dodgy characters, always a gobshite or two. Didn't know about it having been a jazz club. Could've been named for the footprints somebody made in the concrete sidewalk out front while it was still wet. They liked that idea better. Made about as much sense as the name of the bar they were in now. That'd brought another big laugh.

Like it or not, Footprints was indeed just another bar from what he'd been able to find out thus far. He'd hoped to have learned more. Whatever that might've been he couldn't say. Maybe he'd thought the jazz club angle would've been useful. He now even had second thoughts about the gobshite they'd identified as being the shooter. Just another customer.

Miami had brought Astrid Kelly to mind. He wondered how long she and Carl Napier had been living together. Obviously they were a pair. But was it a serious relationship or merely one of convenience? Knowing Astrid, he'd put money on the latter.

He had now come to Duval Street. He crossed it and headed to Harpoon Harry's for breakfast.

~~~

Astrid Kelly awoke with a start.

"Wake up!" a stern voice commanded again.

She was hot and sweaty. It took a second to realize where she was. Cautiously, she stuck her head out from beneath the blanket. A large figure silhouetted by the sun loomed over her.

"Please don't shoot me!" she cried out in fright and pulled the blanket up.

"Take it easy, ma'am," the policeman said, himself startled by her reaction. "Just need you to stand up. Everything's all right."

She untangled herself from the makeshift bedding and reached out her hand for assistance.

"Would it be too much trouble to help me?" she snapped.

"Rather you do that on your own, ma'am," the officer said, stepping back. "Safer for everyone."

She struggled to her feet, feeling a little unstable once upright. She noticed another man was also there.

"Come away from those blankets, ma'am," the officer ordered. "Toward me is fine."

"To be honest, I thought it was a dead body under there," the other man commented while giving her and the skimpy bikini she was wearing a once-over. "Not moving and a foot sticking out. Scared the crap out of me. Didn't hear the snoring until after I'd called you guys."

"I don't snore," Astrid sniffed.

""Do you know this person?" the policeman asked the man.

"Never saw her before in my life. I've been away for awhile. Got back in town this morning and came here to check on my boat and there she was, all tucked in and sawing logs."

"What is your name, ma'am?" the policeman asked.

"Astrid Kelly. That's my boat over there."

She gestured toward the *Justice*. The boat owner raised a skeptical eyebrow.

"Do you have any identification?" the policeman asked, jotting down her name.

Astrid gave a harsh laugh.

"Do you see anywhere I could keep it?" she said, doing a little pirouette. "I can go get some if it's all that important."

"Not at the moment. Can you explain what you are doing on this gentleman's boat?"

"Obviously sleeping," she giggled coquettishly. "Until I was rudely awakened by you. What's your name, by the way?"

The policeman wasn't amused.

"My name is Officer Dale Woods, ma'am, and I suggest you start taking this seriously. Now, please settle down and answer my question. Otherwise, I will place you under arrest and have you transported to jail. Do you understand?"

"Yes," she said sullenly. "I'll be nice."

"Good, I appreciate that. Now, I'll repeat, what are you doing here?"

"I couldn't stay on my boat last night. This was convenient, that's all. Didn't think anyone would mind."

"And why was that, ma'am?"

"I'd rather not talk about it. I'm fine now."

Woods considered the possibility that she might be protecting someone. That was so often the case in domestic violence.

"Is there another person involved?" he asked. "Were you assaulted?"

"No, it's just embarrassing, okay? Can we just move on?"

"You don't have to be afraid to tell me," he said. "Is there someone on your boat now?"

"There was no one else there last night nor is anyone there now," Astrid answered petulantly. "I was alone the entire time. Look, it's not like I committed a crime or anything. It was just a silly thing. Can't we forget this? I'd like to leave, if I may."

Woods exchanged looks with the boat owner.

"That depends on whether or not this gentleman wants to press charges for trespassing," he said.

"Trespassing?" Astrid scoffed. "You've got to be kidding. I didn't break in, for God's sake. I was out here on the deck the whole time."

"You are on his property without permission, ma'am. I'm afraid that's trespassing. If there is a good reason for your being here, now's the time to talk."

She shook her head.

"Just tell the woman to get the hell off my boat," the man said. "I don't want to press charges. But believe me, I'm going to see the dock master about this. They need to pay more attention to who they let in here or else get some better security."

"All right, ma'am. You're free to go."

Astrid gathered up her blankets and stepped off the boat.

"Sure you don't want to take the tarp?" the man called after her. "Might come in handy if you decide to sleep under a bridge tonight."

Astrid gave him the finger and boarded the *Justice*.

Chapter 21

The last doughnut out of a dozen Gleason had bought at Red's remained in the box. Keisha Quorck picked it up and broke off a piece.

"Anyone want another coffee?" she asked, popping it in her mouth. "I'm going to the machine."

Gleason was amazed. She was so trim. How did she do it?

They were seated in an interview room. Quorck had thought they'd have more privacy there than in the open detectives room.

"I'm okay with what I have," Gleason said.

Actually, he hadn't finished his first cup, which had grown cold but the little he had sipped had been enough to leave him with heartburn. He found it incredible that any police station could have a worse coffee machine than Key West's. They should invest in a decent coffeemaker like he and Powers had done.

"Mike?" Quorck asked.

"Sure, I'll take a refill," Green smiled.

They had spent the morning discussing their respective cases and how each one overlapped with the others. And while none was any closer to being solved, they firmly believed that joining forces was the smart way to go.

Quorck returned with three cups of steaming, hot coffee.

"Got you a fresh cup anyway, Detective Gleason," she said, placing it in front of him. "Stuff you're drinking has to be stone cold."

"Thanks," Gleason said.

He took a sip out of courtesy. It burned his mouth but surprisingly tasted pretty good.

"They just serviced the machine," Quorck said. "Coffee's not bad if you catch it right afterwards. Actually, though, I'm thinking of getting an expresso maker. Keep it over at the side of the room. Everybody can chip in for the coffee."

Gleason smiled to himself. This Miami detective was all right, he'd decided during the morning's session. They didn't have all that much in common other than both being cops. It was her professionalism that he was drawn to. She was thorough and could think outside of the box. He had a feeling she could be a tough cookie when it came down to it, too. He respected all of that and looked forward to their working together.

"One final thing," Quorck said, taking a map from her briefcase. "This roadmap was in the Mercedes at the mortuary. Had some markings on it. Probably just directions to past customers' houses but I kept it. Mike, maybe you can tell if they mean anything."

"Not sure I understand about the car," Gleason said. "Whose was it?"

"The key I found on Flores belonged to the Mercedes," Quorck explained. "Thought I told you about this, no? Anyway, I had a quick look inside it the first time I was out there."

"Did you go through the entire car?" Green asked.

"No, just the glovebox. I was hoping to find his address. Didn't have a complete ID on him at the time."

"Let me see that thing," Green said. "Paper maps are kind of quaint. Everyone uses GPS today."

He unfolded it and examined the markings.

"I think we should all go have another look at the car," Green said.

~~~

In Key West, Detective Sam Merrill had just had a breakthrough with his end of the investigation. He'd gotten a hit on a palm smear that forensics had lifted from the SUV's steering wheel. He had earlier sent the print to the state law enforcement department. Back in the day, he would've had to have waited much longer to hear anything from them, and even then the odds of getting a match would've been a Las Vegas long shot. But the old AFIS technology had been replaced statewide with a new hi-tech biometric identification system called FALCON and it was a whole new ballgame now.

The Lincoln's steering wheel had apparently been wiped clean but whoever did it had missed a partial print on the lower half. FALCON matched that with a print it'd stored from an arrest record. Leon Geddes was the offender's name.

The new information had also included a mug shot. It was a close match to the sketch Merrill was at the moment holding in his hand.

But a separate photograph of a crouching tiger tattooed on Geddes' neck was of particular interest.

He had done some work with gangs when he was with the Tampa department. The tiger tattoo represented strength and power. Asian gangs often had them. But the wearer could also have no gang association. Something of personal value. A statement of another kind. The list was long. This particular tattoo wasn't any jailhouse dalliance either. It'd been done by an artist.

The sketch had indicated some kind of mark on the suspect's neck. Now they had identified it.

Gleason was going to be one surprised dude when he hears about this, he thought to himself with a big grin. He sent a request to the Miami department for Leon Geddes' arrest records. He'd also get the booking shot out to patrol here.

Another thought occurred to him. Why not show the mug shot to Jack Hunter? Getting a positive identification from the witness would just add to the pile. Shouldn't take long. He'll ask Hunter to come by to take a look and then he'd shoot an email to Gleason.

~~~

Stripping off her wet bikini and now nude, Astrid had set to work putting the boat's cabin back in shape. Most of the mess belonged to Carl, which she'd thrown on the floor in a mad fit the night before. The job had taken hardly any time. She'd simply gathered everything up and stuffed it in a large plastic garbage bag to be tossed in the dumpster. His few remaining articles of clothing stowed in a drawer also went in the bag.

One item she had kept was a manila envelope she'd found hidden at the back of the drawer. It had contained three thousand dollars. Why the sneaky little so-and-so, she'd thought, giving a nasty little laugh. And here he had been poor-mouthing about how broke he was. Well, too bad for him now.

Now, showered and having applied fresh makeup, she wiggled into a pair of white shorts and pulled on a low-cut blue jersey. Giving her hair a final flounce, she set out for the dock master's office.

She'd called the man earlier to tell him she was leaving the marina. Apparently no one had complained about her foray the evening before and its outcome this morning. Not yet, that is. And not that it would have mattered to her anyway. She would have just brazened her way through and denied everything.

To her relief, the dock master greeted her with a big smile when she entered the tiny office.

"Hope you enjoyed your stay with us, ma'am," he said. "Where are you off to next?"

"Bimini," Astrid smiled back. "May be there for awhile."

"Should have good weather all the way," he said. "High pressure system moved in after that storm. Be sticking around for awhile. Seas are light, too. Going to dock at the Big Game Resort marina? I have a buddy there who can fix you up."

"I'll be staying with friends and will berth at their pier, thank you."

"Whew," he whistled. "Nice to have friends in beautiful places. Not to mention a private dock. So shall I put the rest of the charges on Mr. Napier's credit card? He left it open when he reserved the berth. There was the refueling cost, some catering and of course, the additional docking fees for the extra nights."

"I'm sure Carl won't mind," Astrid smiled.

"Well, thank you for your business and have a good sail to Bimini."

"Yes," Astrid said.

"Tell Mr. Napier hello and you all come to see us again," he added.

She didn't reply.

Forty-five minutes later and safely out of the marina, the *Justice* joined the Intracoastal Waterway heading south and set a course for Key West.

Chapter 22

Jack had been at Harpoon Harry's when Merrill had called. The detective had asked if he could come to the station. Wanted to show him something. And no, he couldn't tell him what it was.

Rather than walk all the way back home to pick up his Jeep and drive there, he decided to just hike it. Twenty minutes later at a steady pace put him at the front desk. Merrill came out and led him back to the detectives room.

"Why all the mystery?" Jack asked.

Merrill didn't answer and picked up a photo from his desk.

"Recognize him?" he asked, handing it to Jack.

Jack studied the picture for a moment and then, without commenting, placed it back on the desk.

"Have you seen him before or what?" Merrill asked impatiently.

"Yes, I have seen him," Jack answered. "Where did you get the photo?"

"That's really of no importance to you," Merrill said brusquely. "So you do confirm that this is the individual you saw shoot Carl Napier, is that correct?"

"Yes."

"Thank you," Merrill smiled.

""Where's Gleason?" Jack asked, gesturing at the empty desk. "Thought he'd be around for something of…no importance like this."

"He has business on another matter in Miami," Merrill said. "I'll walk you to the front desk."

"Looks like a booking photo," Jack said, picking up the picture again. "Is there a name to go with it?"

"We know who he is," Merrill said, taking back the picture from him. "But that's also of no importance to you. Smart guy like you can understand why, right? Think about it."

Jack walked out of the police station thinking very much about it. He understood what Merrill was trying to tell him—that he'd been helpful, they have all they need, don't call us, we'll call you.

But Merrill hadn't understood where he was coming from. He hadn't watched someone get blown away right in front of him. He hadn't had the gun then pointed at him and realized that he was next and there was not one mothering thing he could do about it.

That had made it personal.

Traffic on Truman Avenue was heavy and noisy. He cut over to Olivia Street where it was quieter and continued his walk back home.

Passing the cemetery never failed to bring to mind the children's graves that lined the fence along Passover Street. A sad little stretch of land that had caught his attention in an earlier time and now would forever hold a personal meaning to him.

He had discovered by chance then that the deaths of some of those buried there had been questionable. Rumors had abounded and among them was a disturbing one. It suggested who might've been responsible. Yet, and even more troubling, there'd never been an investigation. He had determined to find the truth and had enlisted Detective Gleason's help. In the end, he'd been left devastated by what he had uncovered. It'd almost been more than he could handle.

The tiny grave sites had been in a terrible state of disrepair at that time, he remembered. Many had no one to look after them, their families having long passed. Now the whole area had been restored. And the entire group given a new name. They were known as the Passover and Windsor babies today. He liked that.

Olivia Street took him to Duval Street and a few blocks later he turned into his lane. It'd been quite a walk.

~~~

Keisha Quorck had been delayed at the police station on another matter that'd cropped up just as they were about to leave. She'd told Gleason and Green to go ahead without her, promising that she wouldn't be long. Green had said there was no need for all the cars, he'd drive and Gleason could ride shotgun.

Now they were parked across from the mortuary waiting for Quorck.

"I'm kind of intrigued with that road map," Green said. "I was thinking about those markings. Numbers and initials."

"Make any sense of them?" Gleason asked.

"Could be dealer locations. Would make it easy to put a dent in their business, if that's true."

"Like shooting fish in a barrel," Gleason grinned.

"Know more when I get back to my office. Thing is, recycling street dealers in and out of jail doesn't get to the heart of the problem. We need to stop it at the source. And that's a big step up the ladder."

"Flores might turn out to have been a good start on that," Gleason speculated.

"Yeah, I think he's a player," Green agreed. "What's more, I wouldn't be surprised if he weren't setting up his own territory. Right under Grubber's nose, too. Man, that takes balls."

"Could be that's what got him in trouble," Gleason nodded. "Hey, there's our detective now. She must've parked around the corner."

They got out of the car and met her at the entrance.

"What happened to your foot?" Quorck asked Gleason. "I hadn't noticed you were limping before."

"Long story," Gleason said. "Boring, actually. Taking a little time to heal, nothing to worry about."

"I'll just let Don Gray know we're here," Quorck said. "That's the Mercedes down at the end of the drive."

A minute later they were at the car and had opened all the doors. Gleason stuck his head in the driver's side.

"Pop the hood," Green told him. "Might as well go through it stem to stern."

"Let's see what's in the trunk, too," Quorck said excitedly.

To their mutual disappointment, the only thing they found under the hood was the engine and all that was in the trunk was the spare tire. Nor was there anything of interest anywhere else.

"I don't know what more we can do here," Gleason said.

"I say we go home," Quorck suggested.

"I wouldn't mind getting back to Key West," Gleason said. "Early start would be a big help. What are you going to do about the Mercedes?"

"Hmm...I suppose I could have it towed to the forensic garage. Let them tear it apart but truthfully I don't think it's worth the effort. They have their hands full with other projects. The cars's not part of a crime scene. Heck, it can just stay parked here. At least, for now."

""Let's keep in touch," Mike Green said. "I'll update you on this road map when I have something. You want me to run you back to the station to get your car, Earl?"

"He can ride with me," Quorck jumped in.

All three gave their goodbyes and left.

Sometime after midnight, a fire broke out in the Christo Mortuary and quickly spread. Everything was a total loss by the time the flames were contained. Including the Mercedes.

Chapter 23

Jack had gotten up early. He'd wisely left the Undrinkable Bar before the Troubled Birds had finished their first set. He had known better than to stick around until after their last one. Otherwise, it would've been a late night. And he had a lot going on today.

The first thing had been to find a place to stay in Miami that wasn't too far from Footprints. After casting about, he'd finally settled on a nice hotel in Coconut Grove.

That done, he'd thrown a few clothes in an overnight bag. He hadn't been sure that the Key West casual look of a teeshirt and shorts would work in the big city, so he'd included a dressy pair of slacks and a long-sleeved shirt from his Los Angeles ad agency days.

A check of the weather had shown possible rain showers returning to the area. He'd decided to put the side curtains and doors on the Jeep.

Now he was motoring northbound on US 1, having just passed Boca Chica.

~~~

It'd been well into the evening the night before when Gleason had rolled into Key West. He had spent considerable time talking about the case with Keisha Quorck before leaving. Their conversation had taken place over dinner. He still wasn't sure how that had come about. But he had enjoyed it and had learned all he would ever need to know about western movies.

"So how was Miami?" Merrill asked when Gleason walked into the detectives room.

"Late," he yawned, sitting down at his desk. "Anything new?"

"Didn't you get my email?"

"Christ, I must be losing it," Gleason said. "I haven't checked my phone since leaving that damn mortuary. Sorry. What was it about?"

"Got a positive ID on a print in the limo," Merrill smiled. "Belongs to a bad guy. Name's Leon Geddes. Your buddy Jack Hunter nailed him as the shooter, too. Just to put a cherry on top."

Gleason leaned back in his chair and closed his eyes.

"Wait a minute," he said. "Go through that again. Slow this time."

"Techs found a palm smear on the back of the limo's steering wheel," Merrill explained. "Someone had wiped the wheel clean but had apparently missed that part. Anyway, the print was enough for FALCON to identify its owner from an older arrest record. Even sent a mug shot as a bonus. Geddes was once arrested for aggravated assault. Don't know the particulars on that. I've asked Miami for the arrest record."

"Uh-huh, and what was it you said about Hunter?" Gleason asked hesitantly.

"Had him come in to take a look at the photo. He's absolutely certain it was the guy who shot Napier. Our enhanced sketch was pretty spot on, by the way. No question now about who we're looking for."

Gleason rubbed his temples.

"Did you tell Hunter the man's name, as well?" he asked.

"Of course not," Merrill said. "He guessed it was a booking photo, though, and actually did ask me for the name but I told him it was none of his business."

"There is a God," Gleason muttered.

"Duty Sergeant has given day watch a copy of the booking photo," Merrill said. "Although I doubt if it'll do any good here. He's long gone. Miami might have a better chance of finding him. We should contact the detective there you're working with."

"Wait a minute," Gleason said, holding up his palm. "We've never figured out what happened after he dropped off the SUV at the airport. Geddes could've bought himself an airplane ticket and flown out that day."

"But what about the gun?" Merrill asked. "He'd never have gotten through TSA with it."

"You're right," Gleason said. "Got ahead of myself there. The same gun was used to shoot Flores. Call that airport security idiot anyway. Tell him we need to see the pictures of the ticket area and waiting room. Ask him if there's a camera at the taxi stand, too."

"He might have rented a car," Merrill said.

"That, too," Gleason said. "Check out the car rentals at the airport and in town. Also, the taxis. Call the dispatchers and ask about any fares to Miami."

"He also could have called someone to come pick him up," Merrill said. "We have to consider that, as well."

"Possible," Gleason said. "But I think he was in too big of a hurry to wait around for a ride back."

~~~

Keisha Quorck had just left home for work. She liked to listen to the local news program during the drive and had flicked on the radio. She'd caught the end of the weather report and the newscaster announced that breaking news about a big fire at a Miami mortuary was up next...right after these messages, stay tuned.

A couple of anxious minutes later, the news resumed and the mortuary fire story was indeed first up and absolutely breathtaking.

Traffic on her normal route crawled tediously. She whipped over to the 95, and though the traffic there was heavy, she made good time and was soon at the Christo Mortuary.

It was an ugly sight.

The rear part of the building looked to be pretty much destroyed. Oddly, the front facing the street appeared untouched but was now only a facade. The front door stood open. A single fire engine sat on the side street and was being kept company by a couple of fire department sedans and a police patrol car. The whole area was still wet and water puddled in the street.

She continued past to the next block and parked.

Getting out of her car, she could smell the acrid scent of the fire. She noticed the Mercedes was still parked in the driveway where she'd last seen it. At least, she assumed it was the Mercedes. Now it resembled an unpainted body shell on the plant assembly line. She spotted an officer sitting in the patrol car and went over to it.

"I'm Detective Keisha Quorck," she said, showing him her ID card. "What's your name, officer?"

"Dale Woods, ma'am."

"How long have you been on duty here, Officer Woods?"

"Since day watch roll call. I relieved the p.m. watch who'd been the first responders when this place went up last night. Mainly, I'm just keeping an eye on things while the arson investigators do their job."

"Hmm..arson investigators," Quorck repeated. "Do they believe the fire was suspicious?

"I don't know anything about that, detective. They just don't want anyone wandering around until they're finished. They were out behind the building the last I knew."

Quorck smiled.

"Thank you, Officer Woods," she said. "Maybe they'll make an exception for a wandering detective."

Quorck went to the back of the building and hailed a person she saw inside.

"Good morning, sir," she called out, holding up her ID. "I'm Detective Keisha Quorck with the Miami Police Department. Got a minute for a couple of questions?"

"What can I help you with, detective?" the man said, coming outside.

"A person connected with this building is the subject of a homicide investigation I'm conducting," Quorck told him. "I was just here yesterday afternoon. Now this has happened. You have any idea of how the fire started?"

"Well, certainly an accelerant was used so it was definitely arson," he answered. "Traces of gasoline everywhere. The lab will be more definite. We've found pieces of broken glass, most likely from a bottle. We suspect a molotov cocktail was used to ignite the fire after the gasoline was dumped on the floor. It's a wonder the whole place didn't go up in one big bang. Whoever did this was lucky he wasn't killed. Fortunately, no one else was inside. The lock on the back door shows damage. Probably broke in through there."

"What about the car in the driveway?" Quorck asked. "Would it have also been used in starting the fire?"

"Other than it was completely burned out, I can't say. Looks like the gas tank exploded, which certainly didn't help."

"We think illegal drugs may have been stored here," Quorck told him. "I'd like to call the DEA agent who's working with me on this case to come have a look after you've finished. Don't know if there'd be any drug residue left after this bonfire but maybe."

"Sure, we're about done here. Fire's completely out. Just watch where you step. Also, this back entrance, as well the front, should be boarded up. Don't want anyone poking around inside. Owner will have to take care of that."

"I'm afraid he's the subject of my homicide investigation," Quorck said. "Maybe you can run down who holds the mortgage."

"The city will have it done and bill the insurance company. Anything else I can help you with?"

"Well, there is uh…one more thing. You said no one was killed in the fire. But since this business was what it was, you didn't happen to run across any…"

"Customers, you mean?" the man laughed. "None as best as we can tell, detective. There are five coffins in one area, however, but I doubt if they're occupied. Could've been a showroom. Most of the interior is burned out so it's kind of difficult to tell which is what without a floor plan."

Quorck thanked the man and returned to her car. Instead of phoning Mike Green, she decided to call Gleason first and fill him in.

"Good morning, Keisha," Gleason answered, recognizing the caller ID. "What's up?"

"Oh, let's see, the Christo Mortuary burned down last night for one thing," Quorck said cheerfully. "Looks like arson. How are tricks there?"

Gleason rubbed his eyes with his free hand.

"You've got to be kidding," he replied.

"Honest to God truth, cross my heart. I'm sitting in my car across the street from the ruins right now."

"This thing is cursed, I'm telling you. What happened?"

"Apparently someone bombed it with a molotov cocktail after soaking the place with gasoline," Quorck said. "Whole building's gone. Everything up in flames. Just a shell of its former self. Mercedes, too."

"This is unbelievable," Gleason said. "I'm floored. I don't know what to say."

"Fuck usually works for me," Quorck said. "The fire department arson investigators are still here. I'm going to call Mike Green as soon as we finish talking. He might want to go through the rubble with me."

"All right, keep me posted. Incidentally, we have some good news on our end. Print match in the limo used in the Napier homicide. Belongs to Leon Geddes. Has an arrest record from your department. Ever hear of him?"

"Not that I can remember. Could've been before my time."

"For some reason, I think it may have been more recent. Haven't seen the date, though. The mug shot is real close to our artist's sketch, too."

"That's good news about the print match," Quorck said. "We'll put out a BOLO to patrol. Check if there's a current address on him. If so, we'll pick him up."

"Wouldn't that be something," Gleason said. "But I wouldn't count on finding him at home."

He ended the call and looked at Merrill.

"This thing really is cursed, you know," he said.

"Well, I'm not all that superstitious but at least we're out of the woods on one part," Merrill replied. "We know who shot the hearse driver. Be just a matter of time before we get him."

"I've a feeling there will be a lot farther to go before we're clear of this mess," Gleason said, calling Jack Hunter and again getting voice mail.

He left a longer message this time.

~~~

Jack was passing through Tavernier and would soon be turning off Key Largo for Miami. He spotted a small restaurant and pulled in, hoping they might still be serving breakfast. He'd always preferred breakfast for lunch and sometimes even for dinner.

There were only a few people inside and he was told to sit anywhere. He grabbed a table near the window.

It was a homey little place and put him in mind of one he'd often gone to near the Malibu Colony in Los Angeles. The waitress brought him a menu which to his delight stated that breakfast was served all day. He asked her for a cup of coffee and said he'd like to have a few minutes before ordering. Ever since Marathon a question had been nagging him. What in the hell was he doing? Since he was now about to leave the Keys, he'd better try to come up with an answer. That or turn around and have a leisurely drive back home.

The chances of finding the man who killed Napier were practically nonexistent. And even if he did have the misfortune to run into him, what then? There was every likelihood he'd wind up getting himself killed.

This isn't some kind of shenanigan he's on. It's serious business and a job that belongs to the police. To his credit, he has cooperated with them at every turn and done all that he can. And they certainly don't need some self-appointed vigilante helping them out. Sounds like something out of the wild west, for God's sake.

He had to laugh at that last part. Especially since it was true.

He noticed a table across the room where three young soldiers were finishing their meals. None of them showed any rank on their uniform sleeves. Buck privates with buzzed haircuts. They most likely had been home on leave after completing basic training and were now heading back for assignments. Could be shipping out soon.

He motioned for the waitress.

"Those three guys at that table," he said to her in a low voice, nodding toward the soldiers. "Put their bill on mine. But don't tell them, okay? Just say it's on the house. Thank them for their service."

"You sure?"

"Yes, and I'll have eggs over medium with crisp bacon and rye toast."

~~~

Keisha Quorck had been chatting with Officer Dale Woods while waiting for Mike Green to show up. The arson inspectors were still busy in the burned out mortuary.

"You'll like this," Woods chuckled. "I responded to a call about a possible dead body on a boat at the Grove marina not far from here the other morning. Turned out to be just some woman who'd apparently had had a few too many the night before and was sleeping it off on the deck."

"Must've been some night," Quorck laughed.

"Yeah, apparently so. The guy who made the call found her lying there when he came to check on his boat. He'd been out of town for awhile. She was under a tarp with her leg sticking out. Couldn't tell if she was breathing or what. Scared the hell out of him."

"I can imagine," Quorck said. "Did he know her?"

"No, he claimed he'd never seen her before. But get this. Her own boat was moored right beside his. Next-door neighbor."

"So why didn't she just stay there?"

"Said she'd been too afraid. Wouldn't say why. I suspected domestic violence but she swore no one else was on her boat. Got huffy about it when I questioned her further."

"Was she from around here?"

"No, she said she lived on her boat and was visiting."

"So how did it finally turn out?"

"Well, the woman was trespassing so she could've been arrested but the man didn't want to press charges. I wrote it up like that on my report. She did have a pretty name, although she wasn't looking all that great at the time. Astrid Kelly. Sounds like a movie star, doesn't it."

Quorck frowned.

"Hmm…now why is that name familiar?"

~~~

Jack sat in the Jeep sandwiched between two large trucks on US 1. The highway had become pretty much a parking lot. But he wasn't in a hurry. He felt pretty relaxed now that he'd made up his mind. The problem all along had been that he was considering the facts and trying to be logical. In the end, he tossed out everything and decided to just play it as it lay. That had never failed him before, he'd figured, so why change.

With a whoosh of air, the truck in front released its brakes and traffic began to slowly move. A few minutes later everything clattered to another stop. It went that way for the next couple of miles. Then for no reason, cleared up and moved steadily.

He skirted Florida City and checked his watch. He would still be too early to check in at the hotel, which was okay with him. He'd just hang around poolside until then. Maybe enjoy a beer.

Chapter 24

"Sorry to be late," Mike Green apologized. "Had to take our dog to the vet. She snuffled an earwig up her nose. Damn stuff's growing all over where we live."

"Aw, that's so sad," Quorck sympathized. "Is the poor baby all right?"

They were standing in front of the mortuary. The fire inspectors had finished and had left.

"She's just fine after having had to blow a hundred and fifty bucks," Green said. "So they think this thing was arson, huh?"

"That's the verdict for now. Let's go take a look. Better put this on. No telling what we might be breathing in there."

She handed him a paper face mask.

"I've started keeping a few of these in my car," she explained. "Leftover behavior from the pandemic. Useful every now and then."

They entered through the rear door. The interior was a charred jumble of debris and wet throughout. The smell was acrid and disgusting, even with the face masks on. Several metal clothing lockers stood against the wall on one side of the room and filing cabinets scorched black and buckled stood across from them. Fortunately, the base of the floor was cement so there was no danger of falling through.

"Christ, I should've worn boots," Green complained. "You okay in those running shoes?"

"I'll watch my step," Quorck said. "They think the arsonist broke in through the back door. Poured gas all around and tossed in a molotov cocktail to set it off."

"Well, that would certainly get things started," Green agreed. "Funny, I don't know much about the undertaking business but it doesn't look like there's much stuff here. I mean in the way of equipment. Not saying what I'd expected to see. Of course, the movies are kind off ghoulish when it comes to places like this. Maybe I'm being influenced. There's a long table over there next to the sink. Wonder if that's where they embalm you?"

Quorck turned her head the other way to avoid seeing it.

"Also, some kind of contraption with wheels on it," Green said. "Rubber's burned off them. Shows you how hot it was. Let's look in those lockers."

Green kicked at a lower one and its door fell off.

"Burned overalls, I think," he said looking inside. "Might've been a dressing room here. No locks on any of the lockers. Guess they all trusted each other."

"There are some coffins toward the front of the building according to the arson inspectors," Quorck said. "Nothing unusual about that, I suppose. I've just never thought about what you'd need to furnish a funeral home."

"Like I said, I'm not all that familiar with the business. Maybe a lot of stuff went up with the rest of the place. Is embalming fluid flammable? Everything in here is burned to hell."

"They splashed gasoline all over the place," Quorck said. "The coffins are metal so they didn't burn. Arson guys figured where they are located might've been a showroom."

"Kind of like a car dealership," Green quipped.

"Pick the model and color you like," Quorck added. "No test drives, though."

"Or lie-downs," Green snorted. "I'm not sure we're going to find anything we can use. Drugs wouldn't have survived the fire if they were stored in a cabinet. Let's look at those coffins."

They slowly made their way toward the front. Part of the roof had collapsed in the area where the coffins were located. Three were on the floor. Apparently knocked off their stands when the roof fell in. One was turned on its side, its top open. Another was battered by something having had fallen on it, the top still closed. And the last was partially covered with debris but seemingly undamaged. Two more stood on metal stands, their tops also closed. They were scorched but they were still intact.

"Boy, these coffins really creep me out seeing them like that," Quorck said with a shudder. "The whole place does. I'm not good with this."

"I'm surprised to hear that," Green said. "Considering your line of work, I mean."

"Hmm…I can see how that would be interesting. Not sure I know myself why I'm so spooked by the thought of bodies being in here. I think the difference is that I view a homicide as a case to be solved. I look at it objectively. Each part is a complement of the total picture. The crime scene. The victim. How he was killed. Motives. A puzzle to be put together. Doesn't mean I lack sympathy for the victim. Actually, I feel drawn to him or her. I'm all they have. I'm their advocate. But walking by a cemetery? Say at night? You'd hear me whistling for sure."

"That's kind of funny in its own way," Green said, "but I can appreciate what you're saying."

Quorck went over to the two coffins remaining on their stands.

"You don't suppose there's anyone inside those things, do you?" she asked, nodding at the closed coffins. "The arson guy said there were no…how'd he put it? Right, customers. Well, none as far as they knew. What do you think?"

"That one on the floor with its top open is definitely empty," Green said. "I'd imagine it's the same with the others. Those on the stands look heavier. Probably made of brass. Pricier, too."

"Hmm…maybe we should open all of them anyway. I don't know. Curiosity? Thoroughness? It's the only place we haven't searched, not that there's all that much left, as you pointed out."

"Might not be a pretty sight if there is someone inside," Green warned. "But you're right. We have to do it. Is there a latch or something? I don't know how you're supposed to open them."

He tugged at the top. It didn't budge.

Quorck gave another little shudder.

"Leave it alone," she said. "I'm going to call forensics. Have someone there come here and open these damn things."

~~~

"Got a minute, Earl?" Jay Halderman called out as Gleason passed by his office.

"Sure," Gleason replied, stepping in.

"Shut the door, would you?."

Halderman paused for a few moments before saying anything. Gleason shifted uneasily on his feet, wondering what was coming.

"Have a seat, Lieutenant Gleason," he said at last. "You've been promoted. Congratulations."

Gleason flopped down into the chair.

"Lieutenant?" he repeated in surprise.

"Came through yesterday," Halderman said. "You seemed pretty busy this morning so I waited until things got a little quieter to tell you."

"This is terrific, I guess. What does it mean?"

"Couple of things. First, your pay grade is stepped up. Second, you get to pin a silver bar on your uniform."

Gleason chuckled.

"What I'm asking is first, how does this new promotion affect me, aside from the raise, and second, what's happening here?"

"By that last question, you mean concerning me, I take it," Halderman smiled.

"In a nutshell, yes," Gleason told him.

"Life moves on," Halderman said, holding the smile.

"Moving on. That's what Sonny Breaks told everybody you were doing the last time. Said you were pulling the pin and moving on. So is that what's happening now?"

"Breaks wasn't completely wrong," Halderman said. "I was really considering retiring. I'd put in my time. Why not leave while I'm still young enough to try something else. Private security work is a leading business today. Several companies deal in it. Good money, too. Or I could just sit on my butt and enjoy life. But then I thought about the department. As you know, Detective Breaks has some political pull in town. He's had his eye on my job for some time. I just couldn't stomach the possibility of him taking over detectives. That's why I pushed you to put in for the exam."

"Yeah, well, Breaks also took the exam and I'm guessing he still has an eye out for eventually running the show," Gleason said. "Why didn't he get to pin on a silver bar?"

"Two reasons," Halderman said. "He didn't do as well as you on the exam and I recommended you for the promotion. The Board went along with me."

"How about the retirement thing?" Gleason asked. "Are you staying with the department or checking out those security jobs?"

"Staying with the department. Actually, there were a couple of promotions recently. I've been moved up a rung on the latter. So I'm pinning on two silver bars."

Gleason leaned back and gave Halderman a long look. Then, and with a big grin, he got to his feet and extended his hand across the desk.

"Well, congratulations to you, sir," he said. "It couldn't be more deserving. *Captain* Jay Halderman. Like they say, it has a nice ring."

"Thanks, Earl." Halderman said, blushing a little. "Another change is that we're no longer just the detectives. We are now the criminal investigations division."

Gleason sat back down, concern laying a weighty hand on his shoulder.

"What does that mean, other than a fancy title?" he asked.

"It's more of a consolidation than anything else. Juvenile's officially with us. That's now Detective Breaks' bailiwick. Also, a special liaison officer's coming on board to assist with other agencies we may be involved with."

"When is all this happening?" he asked.

"As we speak. And I already know your next question. Where do you fit in, right? Same place you are now. You're too good of a detective to become a paper pusher. How's Merrill doing?"

Gleason unconsciously brushed at his shoulder.

"He got an ID on the airport shooter," he said, oddly feeling relieved. "Name's Leon Geddes. Arrest record in Miami for aggravated assault. Don't know much more than that. Detective Quorck followed up but the guy is no longer at the address listed. They've put out a BOLO. We're trying to figure out how he got away from here. Checking with taxis and car rentals. Merrill's on to that. Things are kind of crazy at the moment. Funeral home we suspect of being involved in this drug business had an arson number done on it last night. Just found that out."

"Never stops, does it," Halderman said wearily. "I'm putting out a departmental announcement today about your promotion. Be something in the papers, too. And yes, I'm keeping my office."

~~~

Quorck and Green had been waiting in front of the mortuary for the forensic technician. Quorck was relieved to be out of the gruesome place, even if it was only a temporary respite before she had to go back inside.

"Gleason sent us a mugshot of our suspect in the Flores' homicide," she said. "Name's Leon Geddes. Also included a pix of an interesting tattoo on his neck."

"Why's it interesting?" Green asked.

"It's a tiger. Nicely done, too. Real work of art. Detective working with Gleason suspected it could be gang related. Or not. He said it was also a symbol of strength. Like somebody searching for his identity might find it helpful."

"Whatever it takes," Green said. "Yeah, it could have to do with gangs. But since we believe Edward Grubber is behind all of this it could have another meaning. A guy we have our eyes on down there was a top official in the government. Had his hands in drugs and weapons. Got caught in an anti-corruption sweep but that didn't go anywhere. Politics trumped crime. He dropped out of sight recently. He was also a player in a San Salvador cartel. Name's Juan Botijas. Calls himself *El Tigre*. Has a tattoo of one on his neck. Maybe this Leon Geddes worked for him. Tattoo showed he was one of his boys. I wouldn't mind seeing that photo."

The forensic technician pulled up and parked.

"Looks like it was a pretty bad fire," he said. "I'm Steve Johnson."

Quorck introduced herself and Green.

"So this was a mortuary," Johnson said. "What caused the fire?"

"We suspect it was arson," Quorck told him. "We have to go in through the back. Can't get in the front door."

"I understand there are some coffins in there you want me to look at?" Johnson asked.

"Yes," she said. "They're locked and need to be opened."

"Might not be pleasant. Shouldn't the medical examiner be here?"

"We believe they're only showroom models and most likely empty," Quorck said. "The ME has no cause to be here."

Johnson gave her a funny look.

"So why do you want me to open them?"

"To see what's inside," Green answered.

"We're doing this by the book, right?" Quorck stated, tired of the questions. "I'd like to get going while it's still daylight."

"Understood, detective," Johnson replied smartly. "Let me grab my tool box out of the car. Might have to force something."

"We'd better walk single file in there," Quorck said before they entered. "There's a lot of junk scattered around. Don't want anyone hurt."

Quorck led the way, Johnson behind her and Green following.

"It is kind of dark in here," Johnson commented. "Should've brought some lighting."

Details had given away to shadows in the late afternoon and a pale of gloom had spread throughout the entire building.

"I've got a couple of flashlights in my car," Green said. "I'll run back for them. You all go ahead."

"No, we'll wait here," Quorck said. "Don't be forever."

Green returned a few minutes later.

"These have four batteries in them," he said, handing her one of the long flashlights. "Ought to be bright enough."

Quorck immediately switched it on.

"That's much better," she said, sweeping the area with a wide beam.

"Any particular one you want to start with?" Johnson asked.

"Make it easy on yourself," Quorck told him.

"Let's get the coffins on the floor out of the way while we still have some outside light," he said. "One's already open anyway. Nothing in it."

He knelt next to the battered coffin which was closed and tried to lift its top but with no success.

"These slots along the edges are probably where the latches are," he said. "Takes a key to release them."

"So what do we do now?" Green asked.

"I have a set of keys," Johnson said, removing a pry-bar and a two-pound sledge from his tool box.

A couple of solid hammer bangs on the side and some professional jimmying with the pry-bar broke loose the latches. Johnson lifted the top. The coffin was empty.

Quorck didn't know whether to be relieved or disappointed.

"The other one over there under that mess," she said. "Can you get at it?"

"Maybe we can pull it out some," Green suggested. "Grab hold."

"Must be an elephant inside this thing," Johnson grunted, tugging at the coffin.

"Let me give you a hand," Green offered, bending down and grabbing hold.

Clear of the debris, Johnson went to work again with the hammer and pry-bar combination. Soon the latches were broken loose.

"Think you can open it now." Johnson said.

Green carefully lifted the top.

"Jesus Christ," he muttered. "I can't believe this."

Quorck turned away without looking.

"What the hell is that?" Johnson asked, peering over Green's shoulder.

"Offhand, I'd say it's a motherlode of cocaine," Green told him.

Chapter 25

The *Justice* had berthed at the Stock Island marina after arriving in Key West. Astrid had made reservations while sailing down from Miami. She would've preferred to have tied up at the Key West Bight but had felt she'd be safer here.

Now that she was settled and feeling somewhat calmer, she was reconsidering her situation. Was she really in danger? Possibly she might have been a little paranoid and had acted too hastily.

She ran through the whole thing. Starting with the phone call she'd made to Edwardo Grubber. Well, as best she could. Her memory about that evening was still a little fuzzy.

As she recalled, he had been surprised to hear from her. But was cordial and had asked if she were in town and what could he do for her. She'd stupidly told him where she was and exactly what he could do. Pay the money he owed her. He'd laughed and said she must be joking, that he didn't know what she was talking about. She'd then explained the deal they'd made with Jules Flores on his behalf. He'd professed having had no idea of who this Jules Flores might be or anything about drugs and hung up.

Shortly after that the panic had set it. Grubber might send someone to harm her, she'd worried. Worse, to shut her up. Permanently. She'd conjured up the man in Key West. Look what he'd done to Carl. He could be coming for her. She had to get away.

Well, she got as far as the next boat over. And what a disaster that had been.

Was she being silly? Both then and now? She wondered. There were those strange telephone calls, however. Supposedly from Carl except that he was dead when they were made. Most likely it was the police pretending to be him and were just fishing for answers. They no doubt had his cellphone. Well, so what if they did? They had nothing on her. And as far as anyone knows, she's in Bimini. Including, dear Jack Hunter, who'd just happened to run across her telephone number and had decided to call for a chat. Oh, really? And hadn't that been a pathetic little tete-a-tete. She smirked.

Stock Island was nice enough. There was the hotel and a couple of bars here. Best of all, the marina had accepted Carl's credit card when she'd made the reservation. So she would just live off it there until she decided what to do next.

The only problem was that she had barely gotten here and was already bored out of her mind. And who wouldn't be bored stuck down at the end of the last pier with only the pelicans for company.

How bad would it be to take a taxi into town?

~~~

Jack had checked in at his hotel and was now on his way to Footprints. He had chosen the vintage LA look for tonight. The slacks felt a little tight. He should've tried them on before leaving home. And he wasn't all that sure the shirt was right either. Tomorrow night, he'd dress in Key West casual, providing he was still here.

Parking on the street anywhere near the river had turned out to be impossible but luckily there'd been a lot close by.

He was a little surprised when he saw Footprints. The Troubled Birds had said it was a dump. Actually, it didn't look all that bad. There was even a patio with a few tables overlooking the river.

At the entrance he got another surprise. There were real footprints left in the concrete walk. Not signed, however, like those at the Chinese Theater in LA.

The bar wasn't exactly packed. But there were enough people to keep a buzz of conversation going. He spotted an empty seat at the end and took it.

"What can I get you?" the bartender asked, placing a cocktail napkin in front of him.

"I'll have a Bud Lite," Jack said.

"Want a glass?"

"Bottle's okay. I see a bandstand over there. Anything going on tonight?"

"Lady singer. She's pretty good. She'll be in a little later."

"That so? Maybe I'll stick around."

The bartender left to serve another customer. Jack scooted his stool over from the couple seated next to him.

"Give everyone a little more room," he said.

"You're not crowding us," the man said. "That singer the bartender mentioned. Her name's Leda. She really is good. You won't be sorry you waited."

"Thanks," Jack said. "I'll look forward to it. Is she with a group?"

"No, solo act. Just herself on the keyboard. Mainly does standards. If you have something you'd like to hear, all you gotta do is ask."

"Sounds reasonable enough," Jack said. "Some musician friends told me about this place. Called it a dump, in fact. Doesn't look like one to me."

"Well, it is on the river. A little light industry around. Maybe that's what they meant."

"Knowing them, I think they might've just had a grudge," Jack chuckled.

"Footprints is the best-kept secret in town," the man said. "Everybody thinks all the hot spots are at South Beach, but this little bar has them all beat hands down. Whether it's a dump or not."

"I take it you all come here often. By the way, I'm Jack."

"I'm Frank and this is my wife, Buffy."

Buffy leaned forward and gave a little wave.

"Yeah, we don't live too far from here," Frank continued. "Stop in once or twice a week, especially if we like who's playing."

"You ever hear of the Troubled Birds?" Jack asked.

"Oh, God, yes," Frank said. "They're terrific. How do you know about them?"

"Caught them in Key West. They're the ones who put me onto this place."

"So they're in Key West," Frank said. "Wouldn't mind seeing them again. Where are they playing?"

"The Undrinkable Bar," Jack said. "Another best kept secret. They'll be there for awhile."

He took out his billfold and removed a business card.

"It's a little off the beaten path, too," he said, handing him the card.

"Are you the owner?" Frank asked.

"I'm involved with it," Jack said.

"Well, thanks, Jack, We might just drive down. Hey, that's a cool shirt you're wearing. Where'd you get it?"

~~~

Keisha Quorck and Mike Green were at the forensic garage. All of the coffins had been hauled there from the mortuary and the remaining two that'd been closed were now open. One of them had also been full of cocaine.

"I'd have thought the fire would've destroyed this stuff," Quorck said. "Isn't that how they get rid of drugs? Burn 'em up?"

"That's true," Green said. "Once they're no longer needed as evidence, you burn them up. Some agencies contract the job out. Many have their own incinerators. I think a couple of states just throw them in a fire pit and light a match."

"So what happened here?" Quorck asked. "Hundred bricks of coke tucked away in each coffin and looking as good as new."

"The cocaine wasn't exposed to an actual flame, which would have immediately incinerated it. Guess it didn't get hot enough closed up inside the coffins. The lining there probably acted as insulation."

"Do you see any need to hold on to these things any longer?" Quorck asked, referring to the coffins.

"I think we've got all we're going to get from them," Green said. "That is, from my involvement. You have your own considerations."

"Well, I'll have everything documented again and the department can decide if they need to keep them for evidence," Quorck said. "Or send them to junkyard."

"I bet Gleason will be excited to hear about this," Green said. "What do you say we call him?"

Quorck gave a little gasp.

"Oh my gosh, now I remember," she said. "Astrid Kelly."

She pulled out her cellphone and punched in Gleason's number. He answered on the second ring.

"Detective Quorck, so good to hear from you. What's up?"

"Several things but first that woman you mentioned the night we had dinner, Astrid Kelly, right? I've got a lead on her, if you're still interested."

"I'm interested."

"I won't go into the whole story about how it came about which is hilarious in itself but she's supposed to be staying at a marina near Coconut Grove."

"That's tremendous," Gleason said. "Look, I don't have anything specific on her other than she's the girlfriend of my victim and a possible person-of-interest in this drug business. But I have a feeling she really is in it and pretty deep. Can you find out if she's still at this marina? I'd like to talk with her."

"Do you know if she has any outstanding warrants? We could hold her for that."

"I can run her but I'm certain she doesn't. Just be a waste of time."

"Hmm…maybe there's another angle," Quorck suggested. "It's full of violations and I'd probably lose my job at the least. The way I found out where she was is that a patrol officer answered a call about a dead body on a boat. Turns out the body belonged to Astrid Kelly and she was alive and asleep on the deck. However, she was trespassing. Didn't break in, so it was a misdemeanor. The boat's owner decided not to press charges. The officer wrote up the report. Nothing more was made of it. However, suppose now the boat owner has changed his mind about charging her…"

"No, don't even go there," Gleason interrupted. "I admire the deviousness, though."

"Like minds think alike," Quorck said. "The other thing is, I'm with Mike Green at our forensic garage. We found a ton of cocaine in some coffins at the mortuary. Don't know how it survived the fire but we have it here. Obviously, Jules Flores was setting himself up as serious drug trafficker. Whether Edwardo Grubber was behind it or not, we can't say at the moment. Mike has a feeling Flores was out of his league and stepped on someone's toes."

"I'd give good odds on that," Gleason said.

"Also, I mentioned that tiger tattoo on Geddes's neck. Mike thinks it might have something to do with some drug honcho in Honduras who has a similar one. Calls himself *El Tigre*. Maybe Geddes worked for him."

"The gift that just keeps giving," Gleason said sarcastically.

"I'll check the marina right now," Quorck said. "It's not far from where I am. Give you a call back when I find out something."

~~~

Detective Sam Merrill had considerably narrowed down the breadth of his search. He had looked at all of the airport security camera footage taken at each location from the moment the SUV entered the entrance ramp until an hour afterwards, thinking that should be more than long enough. There'd been no sight of Leon Geddes being anywhere inside the terminal or even entering the building. It would've been impossible for him to have ducked every camera.

There was the possibility that he had hidden himself in the parking area until things had quieted down. Even could've waited in the SUV. But that would've been risky.

Dumping the vehicle at the airport instead of continuing driving to Miami with a dead man in the backseat had been the smarter move at the moment. He couldn't afford a traffic stop. Also, leaving the Lincoln here would've thrown the police off. But time had been against him. His only chance would've been to leave immediately before anyone arrived at the scene. The odds were he grabbed a taxi, probably within minutes after getting there.

Merrill had talked with the person who oversees the taxi lineup on the street outside of the arrival area and had shown him the booking photo of Geddes, not mentioning that he was a suspect in a homicide. Unfortunately, the man had been late for work that morning and hadn't gotten there until nearly nine o'clock. Said he'd been lucky even at that since the police had closed the road. He hadn't remembered seeing anyone matching the picture but offered that one of the earlier cabbies might have. Explained that some drivers like to line up before the first flights arrive. He'd named a few taxi companies and also a couple of independent owners that were regular early birds.

Merrill had started with the taxi companies. He'd called the dispatchers of each one to ask if any of their drivers had been at the airport at that specific time and had made arrangements for them to see the photo, again not giving the real reason for his interest. Everyone had cooperated but not one had recalled picking up Geddes. Next, he'd called the two independents. One had agreed to drop by the police station. The other call had gone to message.

Merrill had stayed late and was waiting at his desk for him. His phone rang.

"Detective Merrill, your taxi's here," the desk officer said.

Merrill gathered up the booking photo and went out to the front.

"Appreciate your coming in, sir," he said. "This won't take long. I'd like you to take a look at this photograph. Tell me if you remember seeing this person at the airport the morning we spoke about."

The man studied the photograph.

"Yeah, I remember him," he said. "Real jerk as far as I'm concerned."

Merrill felt a rush of excitement. This was a big break.

"And why is that?" he asked.

"I was sitting in my cab at the back of the line reading the paper," the man said. "Been there about twenty minutes or so. Not much going on at that time of morning. Suddenly, this fellow runs up from out of nowhere and starts banging on the window. Was in a big ass hurry for a taxi. Told him he had to go to the front. All the drivers are pretty fair about that. Wait your turn. Somehow that pissed him off royally because he gave me a dirty look and pointed his finger at me. Don't know what the hell that was supposed to mean. Then the son-of-a-bitch spits at my car and runs off. Can you imagine that? I started to get out and chase after him but thought screw it. I didn't need the grief."

"Do you recall what cab he got?"

"Had to have been Mel's."

"Pardon?"

"Melvin Carr. Goes by Mel. He's an independent owner-driver like me. Gets to the airport before sunup sometimes so he can be first in line. Lives in Big Pine. Don't think he has any family, so there's nobody to disturb if he wants to be an early riser. Come to think of it, though, I haven't seen him around lately. Does this guy you're asking about have anything to do with that shooting?"

"We'd like to talk with him about that," Merrill said.

~~~

Keisha Quorck wasn't familiar with boats of any kind or shape. She'd really never had an interest in them. But she had to admit the boats tied up at the piers were pretty impressive looking. She couldn't imagine what it would be like to sail somewhere on one. She would probably get seasick.

She found the dock master's office and went inside.

"Good afternoon, ma'am," the man seated at a small desk said, getting to his feet. "Or is it evening? Hadn't looked outside for awhile."

"Either one will do," Quorck smiled.

"How can I help you?"

"I'm Detective Keisha Quorck with the Miami police department," she said, showing him her identification. "I'm interested in locating a person who may be here at the marina. Her name is Astrid Kelly."

"Astrid Kelly," he repeated and thought for a moment. "Oh, yeah, of course, the *Justice*."

"I'm sorry?"

"That's the name of her boat. Really nice sloop."

Quorck gave him a puzzled look.

"What's a sloop?" she asked.

"Has to do with how the sails are rigged. Her boat has a single mast with two sails, one in front and the other in back. Easier to handle than a two-master."

"Of course," Quorck smiled. "Is Astrid Kelly here at the marina?"

"Nope, left us for Bimini. Going to visit some friends there."

"Hmm...Bimini. That makes things a little difficult. She didn't mention their names, did she? The people she's seeing?"

"No, ma'am. I have a buddy at the Big Game Resort marina there. Told her he'd take care of her but she said her friends had a private dock so I'd imagine she'd be mooring there. Must be nice, huh?"

"How far is that from here? I mean, would it take long to get there?"

"Bimini? Only fifty miles. Ferry can get you there in a couple of hours. I imagine a sailboat like hers might do it in four hours or so. As I remember, there was good weather when she left. Storm had passed. She'd have a following sea, too. Favorable winds. So she could've made it in even less time."

"Well, thank you for your time, sir," Quorck said, handing him a business card. "Should Ms. Kelly return, I'd appreciate it if you would call me."

He looked at the card.

"Is there any special reason you are interested in her?" he asked. "There's nothing I should worry about, is there? She isn't wanted by the police or anything?"

"Oh, goodness no," Quorck smiled. "Just a few routine questions I need to ask her concerning a matter I'm working on. Have a good evening."

Chapter 26

Leda had opened with a rousing uptempo version of *Stella by Starlight* and Jack's mind had immediately sped back to Key West. He'd thought of the Stella by Starlight restaurant and Derrick. He thought of the Inedible Cafe and Billy. He'd thought of his life there and the friends he had made. All of which had led him to think again why wasn't he there and what in the hell was he doing here?

"You don't hear that kind of stuff anymore," Frank said. "She's wasting her time in this bar. Should be playing at a club in New York."

The bar had filled up and most of the tables were taken. Leda finished her first number and a big round of applause followed.

"Maybe she needs a better agent," Jack suggested.

Frank shrugged.

"Thank you, thank you," Leda said warmly to the crowd. "Any requests, people? Here's the deal. If I know it, I'll play it. So don't be shy."

That drew another light round of applause.

"She's kind of funny," Jack smiled. "Wonder what her story is?"

"I heard she used to be a regular in a couple of heavy jazz venues out west in Los Angeles," Frank said. "Sat in with some of the monster players. A lot of them were hired guns, you know, studio sidemen. That was a while ago. Can't imagine what brought her here."

"No kidding?" Jack said. "I used to live in LA. Some really famous jazz clubs there at one time. I remember the Baked Potato in Studio City. Lot of celebrities hung out there. Don't know if it's even still around."

"Most aren't," Frank said. "That's why this place is a find."

Leda began the intro to *As Time Goes By*.

~~~

"I haven't heard back from this Mel Carr but I've left him another message," Merrill said.

He was still at the police station and on the phone with Gleason who'd left for the day.

"Told him it was urgent that he call. Since he lives in Big Pine, the sheriffs could run by his house. Check in on him since he lives alone. I'll call them."

"Maybe he's gone to Disney World," Gleason said. "Think the going rate from here to Miami is five-hundred dollars. That doesn't come along every day. Seriously, though, I hope the guy's still alive."

"Yeah, I thought about that, too," Merrill agreed. "Leave no witness. That trick of him spitting at the guy was the same as with Jack Hunter. I have no doubt it was Geddes."

"I'm going to notify the Miami PD of the situation," Gleason said. "They can be looking for his cab there in case the worst has happened. That was good work, Sam. See you tomorrow."

"Have a good night," Merrill said. "By the way, congratulations on the promotion, Lieutenant."

Gleason thanked him and ended the call. Should he wait until tomorrow before getting in touch with the Miami department, he wondered? It's not all that late. Still, it could get lost in the shuffle between watches. Why not let Quorck handle it? She could also get out the word to other agencies in the area, as well. Meanwhile, the sheriffs could run down Mcarr's address in Big Pine.

"All right, Mitts," he said to the cat. "You're in charge. If anyone wants me, I'll be at Vino's."

~~~

Leda had finished her last number for the evening and was chatting with some people at a table near the bar. Frank and Buffy had told Jack it'd been a pleasure, that they'd see him tomorrow night if he was still in town, and had left for home.

Jack scanned the room once more now that it had thinned out some. Oddly, he felt relieved not to see anyone he recognized. He hadn't had any real plan of action if the guy had shown up. Winging it wasn't exactly a winning tactic, though he'd survived a couple of time on just that. He'd better start giving this whole idea some thought before it blew up in his face.

Leda came over to where he was sitting.

He had made a request earlier, a ballad and a favorite of his, *What Are You Doing for the Rest of Your Life*. He had also given her his card, thinking she could be a good draw at the Undrinkable Bar.

"So tell me about this bar of yours," she said, taking a seat beside him. "Curious name. What, they don't serve liquor? Or is the stuff so bad you can't drink it?"

Jack took a closer look at her now that she was in a better light. She appeared to be younger than him but not by all that much. Four or five years. Okay, maybe five or even ten. He'd noticed when he had made the request that she was attractive. Well, up close now and in better light, it was plain that she was even more so. He was also aware of something else about her that he hadn't seen earlier. Her eyes were purplish. And there was an expression in them he couldn't quite fathom. It was intriguing.

The bartender immediately placed a drink in front of her.

"Thank you," she said, and then to Jack. "He makes the best martinis. Straight up and no garnish. But you can only have one."

"I'll take your word for that," Jack smiled. "Back to your question, the Undrinkable Bar is in the Inedible Cafe. And yes, you can get a decent drink there."

"Of course it would be in the Inedible Cafe, which I'm sure also serves the best food in town," Leda laughed. "They fit hand in glove. Is that a Key West thing? Contradictions? I've never been there. What's it like?"

"I suppose you could say that about Key West," Jack said. "It is full of contradictions. Including some of the people there."

She gave him a sly look.

"It's never at a loss for surprises, either," he continued, offering a grin. "That's part of its charm. With the bar and cafe, however, one just followed the other."

"Exactly," she said, slowly nodding. "As one would expect to find in the natural order of quirkiness, wouldn't you say?"

"Exactly," Jack nodded back.

He liked talking with her. They seemed to share the same sense of humor.

A man came up to the bar.

"You still open?" he asked the bartender. "My friends and I got time for a drink?"

"Another hour."

Jack turned to look. A small group of people stood at the entrance waiting to come in. The light was low but there was something familiar about one person standing behind the others.

"Excuse me, Leda," Jack said, getting to his feet.

He quickly made his way over to the entrance and they stepped aside to let him by. He looked around outside. But whoever he'd thought he had seen was no longer there.

~~~

All the chairs were taken on the porch when Gleason arrived at Vino's. The whole place was full, in fact. The best he could do was to jam in sideways at the bar. He ordered a glass of merlot and stood with it in the doorway taking in the scene.

Traffic, both pedestrian and cars, flowed steadily up and down Duval Street. A couple of bicycle taxis peddled past. That brought to mind Mel Carr and his missing cab. He was having bad thoughts about that.

To his luck, a couple got up from a table and appeared to be leaving.

"Okay if I take this?" he asked, quickly stepping over to them.

They nodded and left. Gleason sat down and settled in. This was more like it, he thought, and turned his attention back to the street. His phone chimed. He could see it was Keisha Quorck calling.

"Hello, detective," he answered. "I was just enjoying a glass of wine on the veranda at Vino's."

"Sounds romantic," Quorck said. "I, on the other hand, have just returned from the marina with some information about the whereabouts of your missing friend, Astrid Kelly. If I'm not imposing, would you like to hear it?"

"Y0ur talent is overwhelming," Gleason said. "Let's hear it."

"According to the dock master she's in Bimini," Quorck said.

"No kidding?" Gleason said in surprise. "So she is in Bimini after all. That dock master's sure about that?"

"He said she left here right after a big storm. Told him she had friends there and would be staying with them."

"Any way we can verify that she's in Bimini?" Gleason asked. "I wonder how you go through immigration if you show up in a boat. Not like she flew in. I'm not all that familiar with the island but I would imagine at the airport they'd check your passport and all. Have to do the same for boaters."

"Hmm…the dock master said Bimini was only fifty miles from Miami but I guess that does count as another country. Not just because it's so close but I just never thought about it. But then, that's me. I can try to find out."

"No, don't bother any more with this." Gleason said. "I'll look into the immigration thing. Here's something else that's more important. We got a confirmation, well, as close to one as we can get, that Leon Geddes took a taxi from the airport here. He had to be going back to Miami. It was an independent cab owned by a guy named Mel Carr. We haven't been able to reach him. I'm worried if it's true then Carr might be in trouble. I was going to call you tomorrow morning but maybe you can get the word out at the day watch briefing."

"Have you got any more information on the cab?" Quorck asked. "For instance, if it has a company name on the door and what color it is? That sort of thing?"

"I'm going in early tomorrow. I'll get his drivers and cab license info and whatever else I can find. Send it to you as soon as I have it."

"Okay. We'll talk then. Have a sip of wine for me."

Gleason ended the call and sat for a moment to digest everything he'd just learned and compare that with what he already knew. Astrid Kelly was in Bimini. That's what she had told Jack Hunter. Said she was staying with friends there. Even invited him to come see her. Yet, Hunter had been convinced that she was lying. But he never gave a reason why he suspected that, other than she always lied about everything as a matter of course. Suppose he'd been wrong? Maybe she really was in Bimini with friends. That's what she'd told the man at the marina. Why would she lie to him? She'd said she had been there for a month or so when Hunter had asked her. It's not that far away. Fifty miles. Easy to come and go with your own transportation. Not far fetched to see her doing just that.

He remembered that Officer Ed Stone had indicated that the cellphone tower triangulation pinpointed the calls were coming from Miami. He'd also suggested the background noises could've been boat whistles. Well, exactly. She might have made several trips between Miami and Bimini. Who the hell knows?

He took a sip of wine. That was for Quorck.

Yes, why indeed would Astrid Kelly lie to the man at the marina, he asked himself again. No reason at all. Or was there?

There is no question that she was tied in with the fentanyl. Her boyfriend, Carl Napier, apparently made the deal with Flores but she was in on it. How deeply doesn't matter. Now Flores had been taken out and possibly this Grubber character was behind having that done. Reason enough for her to be afraid.

Looking at it from that angle, where would she feel safe? Not in Bimini, if she's running scared and doesn't want to be found. She has told anyone who'd bother to ask that she's there. It's obviously a smokescreen. She might've been there at one time. Even with friends. But she sure as hell isn't there now. First thing that's made sense all evening.

He finished his wine and left for home.

~~~

"Something I said?" Leda smiled.

"No," Jack said, returning to his seat. "Thought I saw someone I knew in that group waiting at the door. Didn't want him to get away. Sorry to rush off like that."

"That's all right," Leda said. "Guess it wasn't, huh? I mean the person you knew."

"Wasn't anyone there at all," Jack said, giving a little shake of his head. "Well, other than the people that came on in, I even stepped outside to have a look. Eyes must've been playing tricks on me."

"That can happen," Leda said. "Are you just visiting or here on business?"

"A little of both," Jack said, taking another quick glance at the entrance.

"You seem distracted," Leda said. "I hope I'm not keeping you from anything important. Please, if you need to be somewhere, don't feel you have to stay. I'll be leaving myself soon."

"You're not keeping me from anything but you are right about the other. I am kind of washed out for some reason. Think I'd better go back to the hotel and get some sleep. Are you going to be here tomorrow night? I'd really like to continue our conversation."

"Wouldn't miss that for the world."

Jack smiled.

"Me, neither," he said.

Chapter 27

Astrid Kelly pulled up the covers over her head and squeezed her eyes tightly shut but to no avail. Nothing would block out the raucous clamoring going on outside. She would just have to get out of bed and take care of it if she was to have any peace at all.

She opened the cabin door and stepped out onto the deck. Flapping her arms and yelling, she shooed away the two quarreling seagulls that'd perched on the rail at the cockpit.

The offended birds circled overhead screaming loudly. Others quickly soared in, generating a noisy sortie right above the boat.

She went back down below.

The gulls having lost interest, flew away for more promising opportunities.

She sat on the side of her bunk. She didn't feel like getting back in bed. She didn't feel like getting dressed. In fact, she didn't feel like doing much of anything. She was at a loose end.

Last night's outing in town hadn't been the soiree she had expected. It'd been a big bust. To start with, some of her favorite places no longer existed. Had she been away that long? And if that weren't bad enough, those that were still around had changed. There was a different crowd. More touristy. She didn't care much for them. Even the bartenders were new. Not one soul knew her. It just seemed all the fun was gone. It just wasn't the Key West she'd known. She'd considered dropping by the Undrinkable Bar but for some reason passed on the idea. In the end, she had found herself at the Key West Bight standing on the boardwalk looking at the water.

She took off the rest of her clothes and went back up on deck to sun bathe. It didn't matter if she were dressed or not, there was no one at this miserable place to see her.

~~~

"Mr. Carr said he'd been pretty sick," the deputy said. "Didn't know if it was the virus or what. Got his neighbor to run him up to Fishermen's Hospital and have a doctor look him over."

Sam Merrill was on the phone with a deputy from the Marathon Sheriff's Substation. They'd sent him to check on Mel Carr after Merrill had called with his concern.

"Wasn't the virus," the deputy continued. "Although some of that's still around. He said he'd been vaccinated, so that was good. Turned out he had a bad case of the flu. Understand that's going around, too."

"So is he okay now?" Merrill asked. "Can he talk?"

"Oh, sure, he's home. I told him you'd been trying to get in touch. He said he'd turned off his phone while he was recuperating."

"Well, thank you so much, deputy," Merrill said. "I'll call him in a couple of minutes. Need to talk with my partner first. And thanks again."

"Glad to have been of help. Take care."

Merrill grinned.

"That's one piece of good luck," he said to Gleason. "Our taxi driver is alive and well."

Both men were at their desks in the detectives room.

"Here's something else," Gleason said. "Wouldn't say it's exactly luck but I got a little more information on Astrid Kelly. She's not in Bimini like she told Jack Hunter. She's been in Miami the whole time. I called Bimini's immigration office. No record of her ever entering there. You can't just breeze in, either. Have to clear customs, fill out a couple of forms, all kinds of regulations. And get this, if you're coming by boat you have to fly a yellow quarantine flag when first you sail in. Apparently, they don't mess around."

"So where do you think she is now?" Merrill asked. "Still in Miami?"

"Possibly. But not where she was staying. Maybe at some other marina."

"Can Detective Quorck check on that?"

"I think we should let her stick with Flores. I've already called her earlier this morning with some information on our missing cab driver since we believed he'd gone to Miami. She was going to give it to the day watch sergeant to tell patrol to keep an eye out. I'll tell her to call off the troops."

"Okay, I'm going to phone Mel Carr," Merrill said.

"Put it on speaker," Gleason said.

Carr answered on the third ring.

"Good morning, Mr. Carr," Merrill greeted. "This is Detective Sam Merrill with the Key West police department. Been trying to get ahold of you. Heard you've been down with the flu. Feeling better now, I hope?"

"Yes, detective, feeling much better, thank you. I was pretty bad off for a couple of days. Damn flu's nothing to play with according to the doctor. If it isn't one thing, it's another. Sorry about the phone. Turned it off so I could rest better. "

"I understand," Merrill said "The reason I've been calling is to ask you about a man you possibly picked up at the Key West airport. This was early in the morning before things got started. There'd been a car accident on South Roosevelt right in front of the airport, if that helps you remember."

"Yeah, I won't forget that guy. I was first in line. I always get there real early, you see. I live alone so it's easy for me to get away. So like I said, I was at the front and this fellow came up and said he'd just found out his flight to Miami had been cancelled and couldn't wait around for the next one. Could I take him to Miami, he wanted to know. I told him I sympathized with his situation and said sure I could drive him there but it'd cost him five-hundred dollars. Explained I wasn't trying take advantage of him but that was the standard rate. He was fine with it. I just figured he must have money to burn. Some people are like that."

"Do you recall where you took him?" Merrill asked.

"I dropped him off in Coral Gables. Wasn't anywhere specific. He just told me to pull over when we got there and he got out. Don't know if he lived around there. Wasn't residential. There were a couple of hotels. Maybe he had an important meeting or something at one of them. Paid in cash money, too. Fare like that I'd expect a person would've used a credit card or his phone app. Most taxis are set up for that now. Seems like cash is on the outs."

"You've been enormously helpful, sir," Merrill said. "I wonder if I might ask one more thing of you, could you come into the station to look at a photograph? It could be very important to us."

"Sure. When would you like me to come?"

"Soon as possible."

"Well, like I said, I'm pretty much over whatever it was I had. Thinking of going back to work today. Tell you what, I'll drop by before I go to the airport. Should be there around noon."

"That'd be perfect."

"Ask him about the accident,'" Gleason interrupted.

Merrill nodded.

"Oh, one other thing," he said. "Did you happen to notice anything unusual about that accident on Roosevelt when you were leaving the airport?"

"Yeah, looked like a van and some other little truck thing. Might've been a Jeep. I started to stop to see if they needed help but another car had already stopped and my passenger wanted me to keep going. Didn't look like anybody was hurt so I just drove past."

Merrill looked at Gleason.

"See you around noon, sir," he said. "Just tell the officer at the desk you're here to see me and I'll come out."

Chapter 28

Jack had ordered room service for breakfast and was having it on the tiny balcony off the bedroom. His hotel room was only three floors up and the balcony was surrounded by trees. Their branches spread so close to the building that he could almost share some crumbs of toast with the birds.

He'd been in a reflective mood for the past few days. The twists and turns his life had taken over the years had somehow gotten out of perspective and moved to the forefront of his mind. The more recent events were weighing heavily on him.

He needed to spend some time with himself and think about where he'd been and where he was going. And hopefully get a better handle on things.

The balcony had seemed like a good place for the job. It was just him and the birds.

He'd decided not to bother much with thinking about his life before he'd been suspected of murdering his ex-wife in Los Angeles. Although those years were indeed important. Just not relative now and perhaps some parts even better forgotten. Save for Pamela, the woman who had divorced him and yet would always be with him.

Still, memories never do completely disappear no matter how far they recede into the past. He realized that, of course. They lie dormant until called up. Well, the trick was to let them sleep. In other words, don't dwell on the past.

So he was thinking about his present life, the one that began on the day he took up residence in Key West under the ficus hedge on Caroline Street as a fugitive on the run.

And what a zigzagging start that had been. It was impossible to even imagine, much less believe it'd actually happened.

Brownie and Nora had been the first to come to his rescue. They'd taken him in like the stray he was and had given him a real place to stay. Well, even if it was in their carport, it was better than bunking with the street crazies.

Cecil Brunner had hired him at the Inedible Cafe, for the bizarre reason that he'd admired Jack's patience and this legitimized him as a working member of the community. He was on his way, whether he'd known it or not.

Billy Bean became a mentor of sorts for him. And to this day was his best friend, without question.

The family he'd adopted...Ruth LaVere and Bobby Sunshine and Roy, the little African Gray parrot he used to read to from the Bible. How he missed them now.

Detective Laura Dalton with the Los Angeles Police Department couldn't have played a more important role. As his nemesis who had been dead set on arresting him for a homicide he didn't commit and later as a dear friend...and for a brief time even more than that. He still thinks of her fondly.

And there was his return to Key West from Los Angeles after having been cleared and the actual killer arrested. Returning not only a wealthier man but in his mind, a different and better person. But was he? Do we really change? He wondered.

Yet, all things considered, he's lucky to have this life, though apparently filled with bumps, scrapes and near misses destined to follow him throughout.

Like now, for instance.

He mulled that thought over for a couple of minutes.

Then, having had his fill of retrospection, he put a slice of toast on the table for the birds and left the room. Rather than wait for the elevator, he took the steps to the lobby and went out front.

"Get your Jeep, Mr. Hunter?" the parking attendant asked.

"No, thanks, think I'll walk around. Maybe do some shopping"

"Cocowalk is on Grand Avenue," the valet said. "Really nice stores there. Good restaurants, too. Not far from here."

"Yeah? I'll give it a try. Thanks."

~~~

"Don't worry about it, Earl," Quorck said. "Not a false alarm. I'll let the watch commander know and he can tell the troops. Glad your taxi driver is alive."

"Guess Geddes didn't feel the poor guy needed killing," Gleason said. "The driver's coming in today to look at the mug shot. No doubt we'll get a positive ID."

Gleason had phoned Quorck to cancel the BOLO he'd requested on Mel Carr.

"I took another look at Geddes's arrest record," Quorck said. "There wasn't all that much to see. Assault with a deadly weapon. Cracked a guy in the head with a pool cue stick. I asked about it at the DA's office and the best I can find is the case didn't go anywhere. It was dropped. Apparently, the man he was playing with later claimed it hadn't happened. Said he'd fallen off a ladder. Refused to press charges. No witnesses, either, which is kind of odd. Also, the victim no longer lives in Miami. Here's a little footnote you might've missed. Geddes has dual citizenship. USA and San Salvador."

"I hadn't noticed that," Gleason said. "Actually, my partner was more involved in getting the arrest record. I only saw the mug shot. Here's a possible explanation for the other thing. Mike Green told me the cartels were now sensitive about collateral damage. No more shoot 'em ups involving innocent bystanders. Any problems now they handle quietly and in house. Big and small. The assault victim could've been made to see the light, maybe paid a few bucks and was told to get out of town. They were just taking care of business."

"Like it's a corporation or something," Quorck said. "Next thing, they'll have shareholders."

Gleason laughed.

"I wouldn't be surprised if they already do," he said.

"Agent Green believes there could be some reorganization going on with the cartels," Quorck said. "The DEA has their eye on another person down there. Goes by the name of *El Tigre*. Has a tattoo on his neck like the one Geddes sports. I emailed Green a photo of it."

"If their reorganization is anything like what has been going on with the Mexican cartels, it's going to be a last-man-standing deal," Gleason said. "I wouldn't want to be anywhere near the place."

"Hmm...here's a thought," Quorck said. "We have our two homicides which were committed by the same person. Well, Geddes was certainly responsible for yours and most likely mine as well, since the same gun was used in both. But the bulk of the investigation now seems to be shifting toward Mike Green's concern with the cartels. I don't how that might affect anything or what we'd be doing differently."

"My feeling is we'll soon wrap up both homicides," Gleason said. "Of course, Geddes may be out of the country now but he'll show up sooner or later. Maybe the three of us should get together again. Say tomorrow?"

"I like that idea," Quorck said. "Same time, same place?"

"Sounds good to me," Gleason agreed. "I'll call Mike Green and see if he's up for it. Get back to you."

"Don't forget the doughnuts. You know the kind I like."

Chapter 29

"Where's Jack?" Krysta asked. "Thought he'd want to hear this. Is he avoiding us or something?"

The Troubled Birds were at the Inedible Cafe doing a sound check on some new equipment. It was slack time after lunch and Billy Bean was wiping down the bar and keeping them company.

"He's up in Miami," Billy said. "Told me the other night before he went home that he was going there. Wouldn't say why. Jack's a man of mystery, hee, hee."

"Funny he didn't mention anything about that to us last time we talked," Krysta said. "Wonder why it's a big secret? He didn't say how long he'd be away?"

"Come to think about it now, I believe he did mention something about a couple of days. Maybe he just needed a little vacation from that accident. Can't say I blame him, hee-hee."

"I still don't understand why he didn't say anything to us," Krysta said. "Miami's the last place I'd want to go."

"Eee...Krysta!" Tina said, her eyes wide. "I bet he's going to Footprints! See if he can find that nasty little beaut. Remember how Jack was at the coppers? That face he pulled? I wouldn't put it past him."

"What's that Jack's looking for?" Billy asked. "A little beauty?"

"The bloke that tried to shoot him," Krysta said. "Yeah, Tina, I bet that's just it. He got all quiet then, too. You could almost hear what he was thinking. Jack could get himself really shot this time. I'm going to call him."

She grabbed her cellphone from her purse and punched in Jack's number.

"Bollocks, he's not answering," she said. "It's gone to message. What was that copper's name? The one that's supposed to have a fooking amusing sense of humor. I think we should call him."

"The other copper was cuter," Angela grinned. "Call him."

"Doesn't matter which one," Krysta said. "Somebody there should know what's going on with Jack. Is there another number for the police other than 911?"

~~~

Mel Carr had shown up as promised and on time. It'd taken him less than a minute to identify the mug shot of Leon Geddes as the person he'd driven to Miami. When asked if he were sure, he'd laughed and said how do you forget a $500 fare?

Gleason and Merrill had been delighted. A crucial piece of evidence was delivered to their door.

And now having positive identification from two witnesses, Merrill had set to work updating every law enforcement agency from the Monroe Country Sheriffs to the eastern part of South Florida.

"I'm driving to Miami tomorrow for another chitchat with Detective Quorck and Agent Green," Gleason said. "Should be back by late afternoon."

"Hey, I wouldn't mind taking a break," Merrill said, looking up from his computer. "Like some company?"

"Halderman would have a conniption fit if both of us went," Gleason said. "The brass is all over him about the budget."

"Actually, it might be helpful to bring an extra set of eyes," Merrill countered. "Simply to look at things from another angle. Also, I've been shepherding the Rivera homicide. Might be something I could add."

Gleason realized Merrill had a point but he was right about the lieutenant, make that the captain.

"I understand what you're saying, Sam. Just not this time, okay?"

"Sure," Merrill shrugged. "You're the boss."

And there it was, Gleason thought.

His desk phone rang.

"Gleason," he snapped, grabbing it up.

"Lieutenant Gleason, this is the front desk. There's a call for someone in detectives. Sounds in a tizzy."

"Put it through," Gleason said.

"Hello?" a female voice said tentatively.

"This is Detective Gleason," he answered, purposely dropping the rank.

"Oh, thank goodness it's you, luv. I'm Krysta. Remember? From the Troubled Birds? Jack brought us there to see you. We talked with you about that bloke you're looking for that shot the man."

Christ, Gleason thought, he should've let Merrill take this.

"What can I do for you, ma'am?" he asked.

"It's about Jack, luv," she said anxiously.

~~~

Cocowalk had lived up to its promise. Pleasant stroll from the hotel and some pretty decent shops. Jack had killed a couple of hours at the mall checking out stores, cataloging things in his mind that he might need sometime but buying nothing. It'd been fun.

On the way back to the hotel he was starting to feel hungry. It'd been awhile since breakfast. He spotted a small restaurant across the street. The tiny patio on the side looked inviting. It was empty, too. He went over and took a seat.

The waiter brought him a menu and he ordered a cup of coffee while he looked it over. Small birds twittered sweetly and unseen in the greenery.

"Decided yet?" the waiter asked returning a little later.

"What do you recommend?" Jack asked.

"Back-of-town-fish sandwich is high on the list. Fish was fresh off the boat this morning."

"I'll have it," Jack said, returning the menu.

"Fries okay?"

"Absolutely."

After the man had left, he took out his cellphone and turned it on for the first time since arriving in Miami. Not all that many missed calls. Several from Gleason, he noted. One came just awhile ago from Krysta.

He shut off the phone and sat quietly with his thoughts.

This would be his last day in Miami. Regardless of how it turned out. He'd try to leave early tomorrow. It'd be good to get home and back to some kind of normalcy.

As for the rest of the afternoon, it might be nice to spend it lounging at the pool. He'd think about when to head out for Footsteps tonight. He didn't have to be there all that early. No big rush. Leda didn't start playing until after happy hour.

His mind stopped in its tracks. Back up, buster, he thought. He had come to Miami for one reason, remember? He'd be at Footsteps when the damn doors open.

His fish sandwich arrived.

~~~

"Have you tried calling him?" Gleason asked.

"Yes, luv, just now," Krysta said. "It went to message. We didn't even know he was away until Billy told us. And now we're worried sick that he's going get himself hurt. Or worse."

Gleason shut his eyes. He'd should've known something like this was going to happen.

"Either his phone is turned off or he's just not answering," he said. "I've tried calling him a couple of times myself and they all went to message."

"Can you go there?" Krysta asked, "Or send somebody?"

"I don't know where he's staying," Gleason told her. "And even if I did, you realize this is all speculation. He could've gone there for any reason."

"Well, maybe we can drive up to Miami," Krysta said angrily. "At least we know where Footprints is. And we'd be there. That's better than you lot can do."

"That's not a good idea," Gleason said. "If what you're concerned about really is true, you'd be putting yourselves in danger."

"Somebody has to do something," Krysta cried out in frustration. "We can't just sit on our arses at the fooking Straits motel!"

"Okay, okay, take it easy," Gleason said. "I will explain the situation to the Miami police. Maybe they can beef up their patrol in that area."

"But what good is that if the bloke's already shot Jack?"

"The truth is, there's not much more they can do at the moment," Gleason admitted. "They can't just go pick him up, providing they could even find him. He hasn't done anything."

He added 'yet' under his breath.

"Bloody coppers," Krysta sniffled. "Jack's been so helpful to you and now he's just left on his own. Has to wait 'til he gets killed before anyone gives a rat's arse. Not fair, luv. Not fair a'tall."

"Tell you what," Gleason said tiredly. "I have a friend who's with the Miami police. She's a good person. I'll talk to her about this. Maybe she can come up with something."

"I hope so, luv."

~~~

Jack saw a shady spot at the hotel pool and started to drag his lounge to it. The scraping sound caught the pool attendant's attention, who was talking with another guest. He walked over.

"Let me take care of that for you, sir," he said, picking up the lounge and carrying it. "Sorry about the clothing regulation, by the way. New management."

Jack hadn't packed a baiting suit. He didn't even own one. He'd figured he would simply strip off his teeshirt and lie out in his shorts. He had been quickly informed by the attendant that street clothes weren't allowed in the pool area. He'd found a nice pair of swim trunks in the hotel shop for eighty bucks.

"Thank you," Jack said. "That's okay about the other. I needed a new pair anyway."

The poor guy had just been doing his job, Jack thought. He didn't hold it against him. Figured the man was lucky to even have a job considering the way the economy had been running. Still, dress codes at a swimming pool?

"They look good on you, sir. Right here okay for you?"

"Perfect," Jack said.

He took a fiver from his billfold to tip him.

"That's not necessary, sir," the man smiled, waving it off. "Let me know if you need anything else."

Jack settled on the lounge. There weren't that many people at the pool. Small group down at the end. Two women by themselves sunning at the other end. No kids around, he noticed. Probably more new management rules behind that.

He relaxed. A gentle breeze rustled through the palm fronds almost like a lullaby. Soon he was asleep.

~~~

Gleason had phoned Quorck soon after he'd spoken with Krysta. He'd caught her at the police station before she was going off shift.

"I was at the pistol range earlier," she said. "Dropped by here to check my mail and luckily you caught me."

"How'd it go at the range?" Gleason asked. "Did you qualify?"

"Actually, I wasn't there for qualification. Some of us are thinking about putting together a competition shooting team. Thought we'd give a little competitive show for the brass."

"I'm impressed," Gleason said. "That takes real skill. "

"Like they say, practice makes perfect. Having twenty-fifteen vision doesn't hurt, either. So are you calling about our get-together tomorrow?"

"Actually, it concerns something that just came up," Gleason said seriously. "In short, my witness is possibly in Miami right now looking for our mutual prime suspect in both of our homicides."

"Who?" Quorck asked.

"Jack Hunter. I thought I had told you about him. Guess not. Anyway, he's my eye witness. Here's the problem."

Gleason went on to fill her in about his conversation with the Troubled Birds.

"Hmm...that doesn't sound too good," Quorck said when he'd finished.

"Yeah, I don't want to even think about what might happen if Geddes shows up," Gleason said.

"Footprints is in Central District, my old stomping grounds," Quorck said. "Don't recall it ever being a trouble spot. Maybe things have changed since I left. I can ask patrol about it, if you think that'd be helpful."

"Don't bother," Gleason said. "Doesn't really matter. Like I told you, the ladies Hunter brought to the station identified Leon Geddes from our sketch as the jerk who gave them a hard time at Footprints. Hunter also confirmed again that Geddes was the shooter. Now they're worried that he has gone to Miami to look for Geddes. Knowing him, they probably have good reason to worry."

"This Jack Hunter everyone's worried silly about," Quorck said. "And these uh...Troubled Birds... are they certain he's presently in Miami?"

"No one is certain. I've tried to call him several times. Went to message. Never returned them. Same thing with the ladies when they'd called. I just don't want anyone getting hurt."

"I don't, either," Quorck said. "Is he armed? Jack Hunter, that is. I'm sure Geddes has a gun."

"Who the hell knows?" Gleason said wearily. "Isn't everyone carrying a weapon of some kind these days? He's a veteran. I think he saw combat. Some vets do hang onto their gun. Especially, if it got them through some tight places. Not against the law as far as I know. Maybe the military has a different opinion since the damn things still belong to them."

"Well, this is Florida," Quorck said. "You can strap on a flame thrower or a bazooka and it's just peachy. The reason I'm asking is that this could turn into a real gunfight."

"You don't have to convince me," Gleason said. "I can almost guarantee that it will considering who is involved. Even if it's one-sided."

"Hmm…so just for discussion, let's say I'm at Footprints to catch the show and Jack Hunter moseys in. How do I recognize him?"

"Hold on a sec. I'm emailing you his drivers license."

"He has a goofy grin," Quorck said a moment later.

"Tell him to smile when you see him," Gleason laughed.

"Hmm…that line sounds familiar," Quorck said. "Okay, now that I know what he looks like, what do I do? He hasn't done anything. I can't demand that he leave. I don't own the place. Follow where I'm going with this?"

"Unfortunately, yes."

"Right. So the next thing, Leon Geddes sidles up. Now I *could* arrest him on suspicion of murder. But we're in a crowded bar. Might not a good time to whip out my Glock and say 'hands up, partner'. Things could go south in a hurry."

"That's why I called you, Keisha. Hunter being there is just speculation but in my guts I know I'm right about this. He's not going to let it go. And you're right about what you've said and your concern. The odds are that nothing will happen. Hunter will sit at the bar half the night and go home disappointed. But if even by the slightest chance Geddes does show up, Hunter's going to get in his face. I'm drawing a blank on ideas. How about we get a patrol car to park in front of the place? At least that's something."

"Hmm…that's not a bad idea. I'll run it past Central District and make a request. Maybe there's another way to handle this, too."

"I'm open to suggestions," Gleason said.

Chapter 30

The palm frond broke off and crashed noisily onto a lounge a few feet over from where Jack dozed, knocking it askew and startling him awake. It took a moment for him to orient himself. The sun had completely hidden behind the building. Christ, he thought, how long had he been asleep? He checked his watch. Happy hour was already underway at Footsteps.

He jumped up. He barely had time for a quick shower. Racing through the lobby, he took the stairs two steps at a time up to his floor.

In his room he skipped the shower and instead opted for a splash wash at the bathroom basin. He had already decided what to wear and pulled on a tee-shirt Sparrow and Billy had designed to promote the restaurant.

He was out the door and waiting downstairs for his Jeep a couple of minutes later.

~~~

Keisha Quorck wasn't completely happy with this cockamamie plan of hers. Gleason had gone along when she'd explained it to him, though more likely out of desperation. Can't say that she would've done any differently had she'd been in his position.

The truth was Leon Geddes had them both in a bind. He was their prime suspect in two homicides and key to their clearance rate. And that was important.

Yet there were so many pitfalls. She was bound to stumble into at least one. The only hope would be that it was the least dangerous.

She couldn't just cowboy it. But wasn't she doing just that? Sometime that was the only option. You just have to make the right decision then. At least she'd had shown some sense by notifying the watch commander at Central District, whom she'd known when she had worked there. She had given him a rundown on her so-called operation, taking care not to dramatize or make too much of any part and had played down the whole thing, underscoring that the tip she'd gotten on Geddes being at Footprints was specious at best, although she would appreciate having a patrol car in the area.

She had checked over her Glock 19. She preferred the smaller 9mm to the larger service model. It was easier to carry and absolutely accurate in the right hands. She'd chosen the black pantsuit with a white blouse. The coat would hide the Glock and she could stick her radio in the pocket. For a little bling she had put on her lucky gold charm bracelet.

One last look in the mirror and she was ready for action.

~~~

The bar was nearly full by the time Jack arrived. Just a few tables were available in the main part of the room. Leda sat at her keyboard and was having a conversation with another couple. Obviously, she hadn't started to play yet. A single seat was open at the far end of the bar. Right next to where Frank and Buffy were sitting. He wondered if they'd saved it for him.

"Hi, guys," he said, pulling out the stool.

"Thought you'd gone back to Key West," Frank said. "Leda's about to start."

"Leaving tomorrow morning," Jack told him. "Thanks for saving me the seat."

"That's a funny tee-shirt, man," Frank pointed out. "Look what it says, Buffy."

Jack stood up so she could see.

"Inedible Cafe…Undrinkable Bar…Key West…" she read slowly. "Did you design that, Jack?"

"My business partners at the restaurant had some of them made," Jack said. "Help to advertise the place."

"Oh, I want one," Buffy said. "Please?"

"I'll mail you a couple," Jack smiled.

Several more people drifted by the bar. One stopped, apparently to look for a table. She was an attractive woman, petite with closely cropped ash-blonde hair, and was wearing a stylish black pantsuit. She caught Jack's eye and smiled before continuing. He returned it with a lopsided grin.

"I think she likes you," Frank said, nudging Jack.

"Maybe in my dreams," Jack laughed.

Leda opened with an upbeat version of *Have You Met Miss Jones?* Jack noticed that the attractive lady had found a table near the bandstand and was looking in his direction. He could swear she smiled at him again. Then her expression suddenly changed and she was staring at something toward the entrance. Jack turned to see for himself.

Leon Geddes had just walked in.

Jack took in a breath and let it out slowly. Everything stopped around him. He felt nothing. Oddly, his mind flashed to another time in another world but only for a second. It was night and his squad had set up an ambush on a trail the enemy used. They'd been in position for over an hour when suddenly they heard conversation nearing them. Everything stopped then and he felt nothing until the first round was fired.

Geddes had his eyes on the bandstand as he walked past the bar and hadn't noticed Jack stand up.

"Hello, motherfucker," Jack smiled, blocking him.

A moment of confusion crossed Geddes' face.

"Who the hell are you?" he said.

"You're about to find out," Jack grinned.

"Get the fuck out of my way," Geddes sneered.

He tried to push past but Jack blocked him again.

"Stop it right there you two!" a voice commanded loudly. "Everybody take it easy. I'm a police officer."

Jack turned and saw the attractive lady standing not more than five feet away. She was holding up her police ID card. Her other hand rested on the Glock holstered on her side. Her eyes were fixed hard on them.

Geddes quickly shoved Jack off balance toward her and grabbed up Buffy. He snatched a gun from his waistband that'd been hidden under his shirt.

Frank stood to help Buffy but Geddes smacked him across the face with the barrel of the gun. He stumbled backwards onto the stool.

Shielding himself with Buffy, Geddes jammed the gun next to her head and glared at Quorck.

Jack, having regained his footing, took a quick glance at Frank.

"You okay?" he asked.

Frank, his hand covering his cheek, nodded. Buffy began to squirm and Geddes tightened his grip on her.

"Don't do anything stupid," Quorck shouted. "Put that gun down and let her go. We can work out whatever this problem is all about."

"Better listen to the lady, dummy," Jack said. "You've already done one stupid thing. How about trying something smart?"

"Shut the fuck up, asshole," Geddes said nervously.

"The smart thing would be to trade her for me," Jack said. "Want to know why?"

Leda had stopped playing. The bar had started emptying. People seated at the tables were rushing to leave through the rear exit. Panic was spreading.

"Quit talking to him and move aside," Quorck told Jack, her gun now in her hand, and then to Geddes. "And you, let go of her and put down that gun immediately!"

Buffy had slumped and was sobbing. Geddes was briefly exposed. Quorck switched off the Glock's safety and aimed. Should she take the shot? The woman he was holding was becoming hysterical. She could suddenly move in the way. Another factor was cadaver spasm. He had the gun to her head. His trigger finger might lock up when the bullet hit him. No, it was too risky. She lowered the gun slightly.

Geddes grinned as if he'd known what she'd been thinking and pulled Buffy up tighter against him. Buffy cried out and he began to step backwards toward the entrance with her in his grip.

Jack followed.

"Listen to me, numb nuts," he said. "Remember Key West and that hearse? Remember me? I was there. I saw what happened. Without me the cops haven't got a witness. I'm 'way more valuable to you than she is."

Geddes stopped.

"Then maybe I should just shoot your smart ass here," he sneered. "Bye, bye, witness."

"You'll have shoot everybody else, too," Jack said. "Think that lady cop's going to let you get away with doing that? She's probably already called for help. The clock's running, pal. Make up your mind. Me for her. Best offer you'll get tonight."

Geddes thought for a moment.

"Turn around and put your hands behind your back," he said. "Slow like. No tricks."

Jack turned around, giving a little nod to Quorck. Why, he had no idea.

Geddes roughly pushed Buffy away and grabbed one of Jack's arms, twisting it upwards painfully behind his back.

"Okay, smart guy," he smirked, sticking the gun against Jack's head. "Let's go."

The two men backed out of the bar in lockstep.

"Don't try to follow me or I'll shoot this prick," Geddes shouted.

As soon as they were out the door, Leda rushed over.

"Is there anything I can do?" she asked anxiously.

"Stay here and help these people," Quorck told her. "And don't anyone leave this area. No matter what."

Quorck cautiously moved to the entrance. She was sure Geddes wouldn't hesitate to shoot Jack if she pressed him. She waited a moment before going any farther. Then she heard a gunshot, followed by another but that one muffled.

She ducked down and quickly stepped through the doorway and into a shadowed spot but could see nothing. A car suddenly sped out of the parking lot ahead. Its headlights swept across a man lying on the opposite side of the road. She ran up to him and recognized it was Jack.

"You're bleeding," she said.

"I know, I've been shot," Jack grunted, trying to push himself up. "I think I'm sitting on his gun."

Chapter 31

Quorck had first staunched the bleeding from Jack's leg wound with his teeshirt. That'd seemed to slow it down. Next, she'd called Central District dispatch, requesting both patrol and an ambulance come to the scene. She had also asked for a sergeant to come, explaining a shooting was involved and the suspect was no longer present. The sergeant would probably want a detective from Central, she'd suggested. She had been following strict procedure. While she thought she'd covered herself earlier by notifying the watch commander, the fact was that she hadn't mentioned a word of what she'd had in mind to her boss at South District. She'd been working completely on her own and now there had been a shooting. A complication that could easily put her butt in the sling.

Patrol and the ambulance had rolled up within minutes of each other. After Jack had been stabilized, the EMTs had taken a look at Frank. They'd determined that the gash in his cheek needed sutures. Leda had offered to drive him to the emergency room. Buffy, who had been still shaken up, had ridden with them.

Jack had been unable to identify the make and model of the car. Quorck had volunteered to patrol that it was a dark color and a newer sedan, realizing that wasn't much to go on and probably wouldn't be of much help. The detective who'd arrived just as the ambulance was about to leave hadn't questioned Jack. He'd told Quorck that he would save that for later when Jack was more able to talk. She'd said that would be good and had then brought him up to speed on the situation.

Now Quorck was back at her desk in the South District station and on the phone with Gleason.

"He was lucky," she said. "The bullet hit him in the thigh about midway between his knee and hip. It missed the bone. Actually, the wound was more of a rip than a puncture. Had to be painful. More importantly, a little closer in and it would've cut the femoral artery. He could've bled out before anyone could get there. They're treating it as a flesh wound. I don't know how long they'll keep him at the hospital."

"Jesus, he's like a cat. I've never known anyone with more lives."

"Must be at least part cat," Quorck said. "Really had to move quick to break the hold Geddes had on him. Miracle he wasn't shot right then."

"You said he got the gun, too?"

"He was sitting on it, if you can imagine that," Quorck said. "The first shot I heard was apparently when he grabbed Geddes' arm and started to wrestle with him. During the struggle it went off again. That's when he was shot but he was still able to wrench it away. He said it slipped out of his hand and fell on the ground but Geddes ran to his car instead of trying to find it. I explained to the detective that we believed the gun was used in a homicide that South District is investigating and we needed to get it to ballistics right away. He agreed to let me have it rather than take it to Central. It's been tagged and entered into evidence here."

"Incredible," Gleason said. "Look, I'm going to drive up. What time will you be at work tomorrow?"

"I could be here all night," Quorck said. "I have to write the report. Might have some explaining to do. There are going to be a lot of questions, as you know. The first being what in the world did I think I was doing going there alone? Honestly, I'm not certain I can answer that. A lot of people were put in jeopardy because of me. Two of them especially, that poor woman and her husband."

"How are they?" Gleason asked.

"Frank, he was the husband. He's okay. Had a couple of stitches put in his cheek where he was smacked with the gun. No broken bone, thank goodness. His wife, Buffy, was just having a bad case of the nerves. Doctor at the ER gave her a sedative. Should've asked for one myself."

"I might've," Gleason said.

"Look, whichever way this thing goes, let me handle it," Quorck said. "If anyone asks, just tell them that you were passing on some information that you thought might be important. That's all. This turkey was my idea."

"Under the circumstances and what little time we had, there was nothing else that could've been done," Gleason said. "What where you supposed to do, call out SWAT when you saw the guy? I think you did a tremendous job. And I'm with you all the way. I'll leave here early. Should get there around eight. You good with that?"

"As long as you bring some doughnuts," she said, after a moment. "By the way, that was a pretty brave thing your friend did. I believe that woman would be dead, otherwise."

"Yeah, sometimes he's handy to have around."

~~~

Jack was out of surgery in less than an hour. Fortunately, the emergency room wasn't busy since it was still early in the evening when he'd arrived. The other piece of good fortune was that the hospital where he'd been taken was well-practiced in treating gunshot wounds. The bullet had torn through the fleshy part of his inner left thigh without causing too much tissue damage. He had also suffered some powder burns due to the close range.

He had been bandaged, drugged and assigned a bed in the ward for the night. The doctor told him he'd examine him in the morning and if everything looked good, he would be released.

The ward was full but fairly quiet. Two aides eased him off the gurney and onto the bed. A nurse showed him where the assistance button was located and gave him a little pat on the shoulder before leaving.

He closed his eyes and drifted into a dreamless sleep.

~~~

Gleason's alarm rang at 4:00 a.m. Twenty minutes later he was on the road. At that time of morning, traffic was practically nonexistent and he made good time driving up the Keys. There'd been no bad weather to slow down things and after a quick stop at Red's for a dozen doughnuts, he'd arrived at the South District station with minutes to spare.

"You have perfect timing," Quorck said, leading him back to her desk. "Look at that, practically eight o'clock on the dot."

"Been here long?" Gleason asked.

"Got in about an hour ago. Fortunately, I didn't have to spend the night after all. I finished writing my report sooner than I'd expected. Haven't turned it in yet. Like to give those things a second look."

She seated Gleason and went out to get a couple cups of coffee.

"I was going to ask Mike Green to join us like I'd earlier said," she said, returning, "but then I figured this meeting might be better to have just between the two of us."

"I agree," Gleason said. "Have you gotten any flack?"

"No, I spoke with the detective from Central after you and I talked last night. I don't think there will be any problem from that end."

"What a coincidence," Gleason said. "Geddes showing up while Hunter was there. Like it was planned. Unbelievable."

"I couldn't believe it myself," Quorck said. "Want to hear something funny? When I first spotted Jack Hunter, he was sitting at the bar and he gave me that same goofy grin just like in the photo you sent. I almost busted out laughing. Right after that, Geddes walks through the door."

"Someone else with perfect timing," Gleason said sarcastically.

"They'll probably make a big deal about why I didn't have any backup," Quorck said. "I don't care. I did what I thought was best. That woman was petrified out of her mind expecting to be shot either by me or Geddes. I've never been in a situation like that before. I felt helpless. There was one moment when I actually thought I had a clear shot at Geddes but decided it was too iffy. Thank goodness I didn't try anyway."

"So let them make a big deal about this," Gleason shrugged. "First, you were smart not to risk that shot. And second, you weren't helpless. You did what you had to do. You were calm and stayed in control. Kept everything between yourself and Geddes. You didn't push him. A backup would've been a wild card. Anything could've happened. This might've had a different ending."

"Hmm…that's a good point. I'll cross my fingers when I tell them and hope it works."

"Any more news from the hospital on Hunter?" Gleason asked.

"The doctor told me last night that they might let him go today," she said. "I'll call them and see what his status is."

~~~

"Jack? This is Leda. How are you? Is it okay for you to talk?"

Jack had been sitting upright in bed waiting for the doctor. Breakfast had been served but he hadn't felt hungry. With any luck, he'd be able to eat somewhere else later.

"Slow down," he laughed. "I'm fine and it's okay to talk."

He'd figured it was time to get back on the grid and had turned his telephone on. When it rang, he thought it would've been either the Miami detective or Gleason calling. He'd been surprised to find it was Leda.

"I wasn't certain that the phone number on your business card would also be your personal one as well," she said.

"Makes things easier," Jack said. "Thank you for calling. I'm sorry we didn't get the chance to continue that conversation we were having night before last."

"Perhaps we can pick up where we left off at another time."

"I'd like that," Jack said. "I'll probably be released from here later this morning but I have to get back to Key West."

"Doesn't have to be today, Jack. I'm between jobs for a few days next week. Maybe I could drive down to Key West and you can give me a tour."

"I'll make reservations for you. I know some nice places to stay."

"Thanks but I can take care of that. I'm just glad you're all right. Bye for now."

She ended the call and Jack closed his eyes for a moment.

"Mr. Hunter, how are you feeling this morning?"

Jack opened his eyes to see a doctor standing at the end of the bed.

~~~

"Jesus Christ," Gleason muttered.

He and Quorck were waiting in the hospital lobby when Jack was wheeled in by a nurses aide. Quorck had earlier called and was told that Jack was being released shortly. She'd asked that they hold him until they arrived.

"You look a mess," Gleason said.

Jack was wearing the same bloody teeshirt and shorts. His left leg was bandaged at the thigh.

"Sorry I couldn't change," he apologized. "My other clothes are at the hotel. Hello, Detective Quorck. Good to see you again."

"Good to see you, too," Quorck smiled. "You okay to walk?"

"Sure," Jack said, getting up from the wheelchair.

"Then let's all go out to my car and have a little chat," Quorck said.

Chapter 32

After much discussion, Gleason and Quorck had decided that Jack, though having taken things into his own hands that he should never have and which could have possibly but didn't result in a shootout, hadn't broken any laws. To that end, they could see no reason for him to stick around any longer. If he were needed as a witness at some future date, he could be called. As for the present and all things considered, they'd all agreed that it might be to everyone's benefit for him to leave town. And while Quorck had admired Jack's bravery, she'd had to admit to herself that she would be happy to see the last of him. Gleason, who was an old hand in matters involving Jack Hunter, thought to himself just wait until the next time.

The two detectives had driven him to the parking lot near Footprints where he'd left his Jeep.

Jack had stopped at the hotel for a quick clean up and a change of clothes. His leg had started to hurt. Probably from having had to use the clutch peddle to shift gears. Fortunately, there'd been no bleeding. He'd taken a couple of pain pills the doctor had given him and they'd started working almost immediately. He'd figured that once he got clear of Miami's traffic and on the open road, his leg would be better. He'd paid his bill at the desk, tipped the doorman, who'd kept the Jeep waiting out front, and was soon cruising down Highway 1 to Key West.

~~~

"With Hunter gone, that's one out of the way," Gleason said. "Do you think there will be a problem with the couple at the bar? What are their names again?"

He and Quorck were having lunch on the deck of a restaurant in Coconut Grove overlooking Biscayne Bay. Quorck had suggested they go there after they'd dropped off Jack, although she cautioned that it was pricey. Gleason had told her not to worry about the price, they deserved a decent meal.

"Frank and Buffy," Quorck said. "I'll go by their apartment later today. See how they're doing. So far there haven't been any calls from the newspaper or TV stations. Their crime reporters usually check in regularly. Maybe that shooting at the mall last night took priority."

"Well, hopefully Frank and Buffy won't want their fifteen minutes," Gleason said. "Not that they aren't entitled to telling their story or that we're trying to hide anything. Getting Hunter out of the picture was a good move. Turns out he's a damn hero even if he did start things. The press would eat that up."

"Hmm…wonder what's going on out there?" Quorck said distractedly.

"Where?"

"Those boats," she indicated toward the water. "Over near Key Biscayne, see them?"

"One of them looks like a police boat," Gleason said. "It's lights are flashing. Yours?"

Quorck got up and went to the rail.

"It is one of ours," she said. "From the Marine Patrol. Someone probably being reckless. People go crazy in boats. Think there aren't laws against being a jerk on the water. They'll soon find out when they get a nice fat ticket."

Gleason joined her.

"I believe they're hauling something out of the water," he said, squinting.

One of the restaurant's waiters had also noticed the activity and had gotten a pair of binoculars. He stood beside them at the rail.

"May I borrow those?" Quorck asked.

"Sure," he said. "I keep them around. You'd be surprised at the things you see out there at times."

Quorck adjusted the lens.

"You're right, Earl. They're bringing aboard what appears to be a body. Take a look."

Gleason peered through the glasses.

"He has clothes on," he said. "Must've fallen overboard."

"The patrol's dock is not all that far from here. They'll bring him in there. Think I should check out what's happening."

"I'll get the waiter to give us a doggy bag," Gleason said.

~~~

Gleason and Quorck were waiting on the Marine Patrol dock when the boat pulled in. Two officers were aboard and a body covered by a yellow sheet was lying on the deck.

"Hello, I'm Detective Keisha Qourck from South District and this is my colleague, Detective Earl Gleason from the Key West PD. What've you got, officer?"

"Floater, detective. Boater spotted him and called us. Don't think it was a drowning. Seems he's been shot."

"May I come aboard and have a look?" Qourck asked.

"Certainly," the officer said. "Just be careful. Decks kind of slippery."

The officer offered her his hand.

"Coroner's on the way," he said. "They'll bag him and take him to the morgue. You ready?"

He lifted the yellow sheet.

Quorck was stunned.

"Yeah, not very pretty," the officer commented.

"I think I know who this is," Quorck said quietly.

~~~

"There are two small bullet holes in the back of his head," the coroner said. "Possibly fired at close range judging from the scorched hair around the entrance."

Quorck and Gleason had returned to the police station and were at her desk. She'd called the coroners office and had explained that the victim could be connected to an ongoing case and could he tell her anything yet.

"The entry wounds are small," he continued. "I'm guessing a .22 caliber. You realize this is just an initial examination. I'll know more after the complete autopsy."

"I understand," Quorck said. "And I appreciate your help. Please go on."

"Are there exit wounds?" Gleason asked.

The telephone was on speaker.

"No exit wounds, detective," the coroner replied. "Couple of those babies rattling around inside your head bone can do a lot of damage. But like I said, I won't know the extent until I get in there."

"We believe we have an identity on the victim," Quorck told him. "How soon do you think you can print him and get them to us for confirmation?"

"I'll do that right after we've finished talking, detective. We aim to please."

"I have another question," Gleason said. "This guy apparently wasn't in the water very long. Why was he floating? I'd have thought he would've sunk to the bottom."

"Not always the case," the coroner said. "He was obviously dead when he went in. Lungs still had air in them. Saltwater's more buoyant than fresh. Sometimes a body doesn't sink and remains on the surface. Funny thing about drownings. They're all different. I could talk about them all day but like they say, time's a'wasting."

"Thank you, sir," Quorck said. "We'll get out of your hair and wait for your report."

Quorck ended the call.

"That guy thinks he's a card," Gleason said dryly.

"There's no question it's Geddes," Quorck said. "Look at that tattoo."

She had taken pictures of the body with her cellphone before the coroner's team had arrived and had downloaded them into her computer.

"I'd like for Mike Green to see that," Gleason said. "No doubt this was an execution. But why?"

"Can you stick around a little longer?" Quorck asked. "I'll give Mike a call."

"Go ahead. I'll grab us a cup of coffee."

"He's on his way," Quorck said when Gleason returned.

Twenty minutes later the front desk called to say Green was there. Quorck went out to bring him back.

"Sounds like you two have been busy since I was last here," Green said.

"We have been but maybe you can help us find out where we are in the wilderness," Gleason grinned.

"Leon Geddes was murdered," Quorck said. "We just spoke with the coroner. He hadn't begun a full autopsy but was able to tell us a little about the wounds. Two of them in the back of the head at close range. Probably made by a .22 caliber bullet."

"A .22 gets the job done nice and neat," Green said. "Doesn't make much noise, either."

"Show him the tattoo picture, Keisha," Gleason said.

"It's a closeup of his neck," Quorck explained, scrolling to the photograph of Leon Geddes. "There was an indication of a similar one in his booking picture."

"Looks like he was with *El Tigre*," Green said. " Nasty little group put together by Juan Botijas. Remember, I told you about him being a big player in Honduras? Things haven't gone well for him lately. The court there recently confirmed an extradition request to send his sorry ass back here on weapon and drug charges. Now things have really gone bad. Found him yesterday in his car with a bullet in his head. Don't know the caliber."

"Any idea who's behind it?" Gleason asked.

"We talked about the shakeup in the Mexican cartels," Green said. "A regular war down there. It's spilling over into other countries, too. But I think this might've been another example of taking care of business. Edwardo Grubber runs the Columbian's pipeline from Honduras to the USA. Juan Botijas had a finger in the works as well, only maybe just a pinky. With him soon off to the States for a possible trial he became a liability."

"But what about Geddes?" Gleason asked.

"Yeah, good question," Green said. "We know that Botijas was running his own show in Miami. Whether he had permission from Grubber or not, that we don't know. But he might've made a deal with Jules Flores who was already trafficking here and they cooked up the fentanyl plan. Geddes worked for Botijas more likely as muscle. Remember that map we found in the Mercedes? A lot of those locations were drop-offs. Things just fell apart with that hearse accident. Grubber got wind of what was going on and pulled the plug on them. Like I said earlier, taking care of business."

"Christ, what a mess," Gleason said.

"I don't think we'll ever know the full story," Green said.

"Well, Geddes clears the Napier homicide," Gleason said. "Same with Flores, right, Keisha?"

"I suppose so," Quorck agreed. "It's circumstantial but the gun that shot him belonged to Geddes. That's pretty compelling evidence. But who shot Geddes?"

"Maybe the same person who helped him kill Flores," Green suggested.

"I think that one will probably go to a cold case," Quorck said wearily.

"When are you heading back to Key West, Earl?" Green asked.

"Soon as we're done here."

Chapter 33

Jack ran into serious stop-and-go traffic just before reaching Marathon, and from there on until outside of Boca Chica where the traffic finally picked up.

His leg was killing him. At Stock Island he decided to turn off and give it a rest. The lounge on the aft deck of the *Joyful Noise* would be more comfortable than the Jeep's seat. Maybe there'd be something cold to drink in the fridge as well.

Although it'd been a long drive, there was still plenty of light left in the day. He parked the Jeep and walked to the marina where the boat was docked. He was careful not to throw a leg over the rail and hop aboard. Instead he used the tiny gangplank.

Lying on his back in the chaise lounge, he thought that maybe he'd just spend the night right here. There was no real rush to get back to his house.

He noticed some activity on another boat at the end of the pier. It looked like it was preparing to cast off. He sat up and took another look.

It wasn't just any boat. It was the *Justice*.

And yes, she was readying to leave. In fact, there was Astrid Kelly herself on deck dropping the bow line.

He'd known all along that she wasn't in Bimini. Probably been here the whole time. Gleason should know about this. He reached for his cellphone.

Then he hesitated.

What good would it do to tell Gleason? Could he have the Coast Guard stop her? He supposed he could but then what? While most likely she was connected with the drugs, there were no witnesses to prove it. And she had nothing to do with the homicide. He was the witness to that.

The last mooring line fell and the *Justice* began to move slowly into the channel under power. Jack watched as she picked up speed and entered the open waters. The sails filled and the boat heeled over on course and was soon out of sight, and hopefully, out of his life...

He sat for a moment and then got up. He decided not to spend the night here after all but would continue on home.

Fifteen minutes later, he was waiting at the stoplight where US 1 intersects with South Roosevelt Boulevard. The last time he'd been at this very corner he'd turned left to go past the airport and his life took a turn he wished he'd have missed.

The light changed and he turned right.

The End

Thank you for reading. Please review this book. Reviews help others find Absolutely Amazing eBooks and inspire us to keep providing these marvelous tales.

If you would like to be put on our email list to receive updates on new releases, contests, and promotions, please go to AbsolutelyAmazingEbooks.com and sign up.

About the Author

Robert Coburn is originally from Norfolk, Virginia. After high school in Norfolk, he spent three years in the US Army as a helicopter crew chief stationed in Berlin, Germany. He returned home to attend college at Richmond Professional Institute (Now VCU) in Richmond, Virginia, where he earned a Bachelor of Science degree in Advertising. He also met his wife in Richmond while a student there.

Coburn has worked at major advertising agencies in New York and Los Angeles. His ads have won top awards both nationally and internationally. He is an instrument rated commercial pilot and plays saxophone. He and his wife now live in Carmel, California.